'Pa, I tell you, he's a wash
A down-an'-out. Nothin'.

Herne the . . . Herne the . . . Cyrus's mind raced as he clenched the nails of his fingers tight into his hand and sweat pumped from the pores of his body.

'Pa.'

Behind them, Tom Lenegan's body made a final pitch to the ground. The sound drew Herne's attention, his eyes flickered away and Hal saw his chance. Seized it. Seized the gun at his hip and rocked his body back as the gun came up, the hammer moving smoothly back as it swung through the angle, a smile bordering on the older son's mouth – easy, easy, easy: nothing but an old tramp – finger tightening on the trigger.

'Herne the Hunter!' The name leapt aloud from Cyrus's lips as the memory shot home.

Also by John J. McLaglen

HERNE THE HUNTER: WHITE DEATH
HERNE THE HUNTER: RIVER OF BLOOD
HERNE THE HUNTER: THE BLACK WIDOW
HERNE THE HUNTER: SHADOW OF THE VULTURE
HERNE THE HUNTER: APACHE SQUAW
HERNE THE HUNTER: DEATH IN GOLD
HERNE THE HUNTER: CROSS-DRAW
HERNE THE HUNTER: MASSACRE
HERNE THE HUNTER: VIGILANTE!
HERNE THE HUNTER: SILVER THREADS
HERNE THE HUNTER: SUN DANCE
HERNE THE HUNTER: BILLY THE KID
HERNE THE HUNTER: DEATH SCHOOL

and published by Corgi Books

John J. McLaglen

Herne The Hunter 15: Till Death

CORGI BOOKS
A DIVISION OF TRANSWORLD PUBLISHERS LTD

HERNE THE HUNTER 15: TILL DEATH
A CORGI BOOK 0 552 11585 1

First publication in Great Britain

PRINTING HISTORY
Corgi edition published 1981

This book is set in 10 on 11½pt Intertype Baskerville

Corgi Books are published by Transworld Publishers Ltd.,
Century House, 61-63 Uxbridge Road,
Ealing, London W5 5SA
Printed and bound in Great Britain by
©ollins, Glasgow

for Lorraine and Mike:
it doesn't have to end this way.

I take thee to my wedded wife
to have and to hold
from this day forward
for better, for worse
for richer, for poorer
in sickness and in health
to love and to cherish
till death us do part

Chapter One

Tom Lenegan had not left Katie more than a half-hour when the first Indian appeared. He ran, bent-backed, along twenty feet of flat red rock, jumped a crevice and disappeared from sight. Apache. Even though he didn't see him for perhaps a mile, Tom knew he was still there. He knew he could reckon on seeing him again. His hand went automatically to the pistol at his belt, slipping the safety thong from the hammer and drawing the weapon clear so's he could check the load. His fingers performed the actions almost without thinking – his thoughts were for Katie. If the Apache were off the reservation then it was well that they were following him and not her. She would have had no more than a fifteen-minute drive back in her rig from the grove of aspens where they'd met, to the ranch house she shared with her family.

He was of half a mind to round on his tracks and go back to her, but better judgement prevented him. For one thing, if there was a band of Apache keeping him company then he'd only succeed in drawing them back towards her. For another, rushing into the ranch to Katie's rescue wouldn't be the most tactful thing he could do. Not when they'd been meeting in secret, snatching moments. Not when Katie had said at last, 'Yes, all right, I'll tell my pa – tell him. I promise.'

Tom remembered her face when she said that, her eyes bright yet anxious, a slight tremble of the lip as her hand caught his arm and gripped it tight.

'I'll tell him.'

Then the second Apache showed himself, across the trail and ahead. This one seated on a piebald pony, war lance in one hand and trailing almost to the ground. He was wearing a dark red shirt, a strip of blue cloth fast round his head and lank black hair tumbling past his shoulders. Just sitting there, watching. And at his left the same Indian he'd seen first – the same by the old army jacket he wore, one sleeve hanging loose at the shoulder, baggy tan pants – running silently from rock to rock.

Tom Lenegan's left hand touched the stock of his Winchester, as much for reassurance as anything else.

How many of them, he thought, how many?

He hadn't heard in town of any Apache jumping the reservation in the past few days, though it was a common enough occurrence. Tom could understand why. The Indians had been deprived of everything they needed to live; they were forced to stand in line for the simplest supplies, lines that were long and humiliating and to the Apache futile. At the end of it you got flour or bacon or perhaps a section of beef that was already beginning to stink and collect tiny flies inside its fibres. You couldn't get self-respect. The reservation didn't have it in stock. Not ever.

Tom could see what the Apaches were doing, jumping the reservation. That didn't mean he condoned what they did once they were free: nor what they'd done before the Army fenced them in. He certainly wasn't about to lay down his life for the principle of it; he wasn't going to let them have his horse and guns either, which was probably what they were interested in. Not himself.

Three now. The one to his left had gained a friend. The red-shirt on the piebald was riding along, keeping just ahead and now not bothering to look back to see where Tom was.

Four.

If they kept popping up like gophers there'll damn soon be a whole tribe of them.

Of course, they hadn't made a hostile move as yet, but Tom didn't imagine they were keeping him company for the pleasure of it. As if to prove his point, both flanks began slowly to converge. Tom gulped a mouthful of air and readied himself. The horse he was riding was a good one, two years old, strong – might outrace the whole bunch of them and that would settle things easier than . . .

Tom kicked his spurs into the horse's sides and hollered for him to go. He slapped the reins this way and that and slid his body low in the saddle, calling again in the animal's ear. Already he could hear sounds of pursuit. Almost too late he noticed that a red-faced chunk of rock was pushing out across the trail and that the Indian atop it was perched ready to spring.

As Tom's horse sped towards the rock, the Apache pushed himself off powerful legs, axe in hand, leaping out. Tom jerked the rein awkwardly, throwing himself across to the other side of his saddle, left boot sliding easily from the stirrup.

Something powerful and hard smashed against his left knee and the Apache had hold of the bridle with one hand and was running with the horse, feet skipping on the hard ground as he tried to haul himself up on to the animal's back or pull Tom off.

Tom twisted sideways and jabbed his elbow hard into the Apache's face. He missed, tried again, missed and struck his shoulder, again and felt something that might have been the Indian's nose give under the blow. Tom ducked as a flailing swing with the axe swished above his head and he pulled his pistol from its holster and tried to fire at the Apache from beneath his left arm. The speed of the horse, the jolting caused by the Indian, made certain that he missed. The Apache managed to get one leg over the animal's rump. Tom pressed the barrel end of his gun against the Indian's left arm and fired. A roar of pain seemed so close that for a moment he imagined it had come from his own mouth. And then the fingers loosed their hold on the bridle, Tom glimpsed the movement of a brown arm jetted with blood, and the Apache was a sprawling heap on the ground, covering his head with his arms to protect himself from the pony hoofs that galloped over and around him.

Tom's breath was tight in his throat.

He willed himself to look over his shoulder but twenty, thirty yards were swallowed before he did so. Five Indians, the red-shirted one in the front of the bunch, brandishing his spear. One of the others was naked to the waist, a vermillion streak of paint slashed diagonally across his chest like some grotesque wound. Tom saw the brave with the torn Army jacket begin to swing wide, one of the others following him.

He turned ahead and saw why. The land was flattening out, the rocks which had bordered the trail were diminishing. Ahead was desert, a brown-grey wasteland from which giant Saguaro cactuses rose up like giant, upthrust hands. The tops of the fingers were beginning to break open in flower; tips of white showed fleetingly against the green.

Tom glanced back: he was holding his ground but certainly not gaining. If the Apache had guns they would have used them by now, he was sure. As long as his horse kept going, as long as the gap separating them remained the same, he would be all right.

Three miles of this desert until the next range of hills and after that the landscape began its dramatic change. The river that fed the San Pedro watered a valley that was thick with aspens and firs on its sides and which held some of the best farmland he knew close by the base. Jesus! Tom knew that valley inch by inch, near enough blade of grass by blade of grass. He knew the fall of the land and the coldness of the stream and he knew the exact spot he'd picked out for Katie and himself to live. Down at the far end from his folks. Three miles of desert and it was going to be the longest three miles of Tom Lenegan's life.

The pair of braves who'd spun out to the east were turning in again, driving their ponies as hard as they could and trying to cut him off. Red-shirt was yelling and screaming and waving his lance like a fury. They wanted him bad, wanted his rifle and six-gun and horse.

Damn them!

Tom drew the pistol again and tried to steady his arm along the horse's neck. He gritted his teeth and squinted, sun behind him; the arm jolted as he fired and the bullet passed over the heads of the Apaches by more than a man's height.

Damn!

Tom swivelled in the saddle and took a shot at the red-shirt and then cursed himself twice – one time for missing and another for wasting ammunition when it might be the most precious thing he had. 'Cause if he didn't outrace them across that patch of cactus-studded scrub and sand then he was going to be needing every bullet.

Tom pushed the gun down into his holster and whipped up the horse some more with the reins.

'Come on, you beauty! Come on, let's give these bastards the back of my ass!' Tom patted the animal's neck as he leaned over it. 'Yours too!'

The Apache in the Army coat was less than ten yards to Tom's left and closing fast. The brave with him was another five yards behind him. The piebald – a hasty check over his shoulder – was no more than twenty yards at back. It wasn't happening. He wasn't getting away. He wasn't even holding his own any more. Another quarter of a mile, less, and they would be up to him.

Tom's throat was prickly-dry; his shirt was sticking to his body at the back and under his armpits. His stomach felt hollow with gathering fear.

He swayed to the left, drew his pistol and swayed back again, turning the upper half of his body. He straightened his arm and aimed the gun at the Apache in the Army coat. The shot went wide, speeding between the two Indians.

'Jesus Christ!'

Tom fired again, knowing as he was doing so that it was too fast, snatched rather than squeezed.

To his amazement the second of the two Apaches threw

both arms up into the air and rocked backwards on the striped blanket thrown over the pony's back. For several more moments he held himself there with his knees but then went back, somersaulting over the pony's rump. It hadn't been the one he was aiming for but it counted just the same.

What it didn't do was stop the rider closing on him with each fresh stride and now beginning to swing the axe with his right arm, wide curving swings which threatened to cleave Tom's head almost from his shoulders. Tom rested the gun barrel on his left forearm. He could see the dark shine of the Apache's eyes, the lines of his face, the hatred that showed in the set of his mouth, the muscular force of the arm, the edge of the axe.

Tom squeezed the trigger.

Nothing seemed to happen other than the roar of the explosion.

Five yards separated them.

Four.

Two.

The Apache's mouth opened and Tom stared at tongue and teeth and as he stared a gobbet of blood flew from the Indian's mouth and landed on the pony's neck. The Apache began to sway from side to side. Tom let his head turn further. The remaining three were the same distance behind as before.

The Apache in the Army jacket was rocking from left to right but wouldn't fall. The axe made one attempt to rise through a last murderous arc but when it was level with the brave's leg it slipped from his failing fingers and bounced along the dry ground until it was still. The Apache was keeping himself in the saddle by instinct; his hands no longer held the rope which led from the hide bridle; his legs were no longer tight about the pony's sides. His eyes were closed. Tom knew it was useless to watch him any more but he could not stop. He was fascinated.

Finally the Indian toppled slowly sideways and pitched head first to the desert floor.

Tom looked back. He seemed to have pulled another five yards from his pursuers. The first traces of a smile showed at the corners of his mouth and at the back of his eyes. He had known all along it would be all right. Didn't it have to be, after Katie had agreed to tell her pa, tell him that they wanted to be wed?

Didn't it?

Tom Lenegan rocked his body in the saddle and urged the horse on with spurs and reins and voice and in the midst of that he heard the first stretch and break of leather.

Panic flooded his mind.

A week ago he'd been in the barn with his young cousin come to stay on a visit. They'd been fooling around and play-fighting the way they'd always done since knee-high to a cricket. His cousin had pulled down a saddle and harness from the rail and only later, replacing it, had the weakening of the girth been noticed.

'Best look to that, Tom, else you'll go ass over tip afore you know it.'

And his cousin had run, laughing, from the barn.

'Best look to that, Tom.'

Tom kicked his heels hard down into the animal's flanks. The leather groaned and tore. He felt the saddle immediately slide to the left and struggled to right himself, pressing with his boots down at the stirrup irons, somehow thinking to keep himself aright.

The chasing Apaches were only ten yards to his rear.

The girth slipped round; the saddle pitched sideways; the stirrups swung. Tom grabbed at the horse's neck and fought to remain on its back while the saddle fell out from underneath him. Holding . . . holding . . .

He went with the saddle, crashing to the ground. Pony hoofs thudded round his head. Just as the Indian he had shot had tried to do, Tom's arms wound about his head, he pulled his knees to his chest and made himself as small as possible. His fall had been too sudden, too unexpected for the Indians to react. All three rode past and then tried to turn their ponies so as to round upon him before he could recover.

His body conscious of the danger, Tom responded fast. He uncurled and moved into a crouch. His pistol had been shaken from its holster and had fallen some way out of reach over to the right. His rifle was with the saddle, several yards behind him. Tom turned and jumped backwards, hands reaching for the Winchester and grabbing at its stock. He landed beside the saddle and rolled half on to his back, tugging the rifle clear of the long scabbard as the Apaches charged in.

Up on one knee, Tom levered a shell into the chamber.

Red-shirt was over him, the lance whirling like a silvered blur through the air. The point shimmered, star-like, in the rays of the sun. Tom felt the wind of it as it passed alongside his right cheek.

He brought the Winchester up six inches and fired; levered and fired; levered and fired. Sprang around, levered and fired. One of the Apache lay on his back with a bullet wound high in his chest, blood pulsing greedily on to a shirt that was thick and stiff with grease. At that moment, Tom didn't know if he had hit the third brave or not. Ponies seemed to whirl about him, close. Dust and sand choked his eyes, clogged his mouth. There was another flash of light and he knew it was the lance and he dived aside, rolling fast. Hoofs thundered by him so near that they seemed to be inside his head. He was struck on the left shoulder and shouted and rolled and then tried to get to his feet. He fell back. Unable to understand why, he glanced down and saw dark red on the top of his pants; if he had been wounded he knew neither how nor when.

A scream of defiance broke from Tom's lips as he saw red-shirt galloping in: Tom grasped the rifle in both hands and thrust it up above his head as the lance came shuddering down. Arms outstretched, the blow vibrated the length of his body, echoed down his spine. The blade of the lance split asunder. The Apache was past.

Tom heard a fresh sound and dropped on to his belly as a hatchet carved the space where he had been seconds before.

Bringing up the rifle he put two bullets into the Apache's back. The brave's pony carried on its mad gallop and its rider spread his legs wider and seemed to sit on the air for longer than was possible.

As the Indian pitched downwards, Tom turned again and saw that the remaining Apache was returning. This time he was lying over the side of the pony, all of his body shielded save for a hand and a foot. The piebald came at Tom almost head-on and he sweated and held his breath and looked along the barrel for something to aim at. Closer and closer. Tom bit down into his lower lip and shot at the pony's head. The animal swerved violently aside. Tom levered a fresh shell and tried for the Apache, the bullet grazing a line down the pony's back. He . . . the gun was empty.

The pony made a half-circle, hesitated, folded its front legs neatly and collapsed.

Red-shirt leapt over the dying body of the pony and came at Tom headlong, pulling a knife from a beaded sheath at his side. Tom stood with legs braced and reversed the Winchester. As the Apache got to within five yards, Tom began his swing. The lunge with the knife was sooner, quicker than he'd anticipated. The Apache was inside the swirl of the rifle, the butt went behind his head as he ducked underneath it, and Tom was forced to hurl himself backwards, letting go of the weapon as he did so. His chest burnt him, suddenly, vividly, burnt him. As he went down he kicked up with his right leg and felt the shin connect with something solid. Tom's eyes were filled with dust and his thigh screamed to his brain and he felt rather than saw the Apache's blow. His left arm went up to block, succeeded in halting the blade less than twelve inches from his face. Tom jumped at the Indian, butting the crown of his head into the Apache's stomach. With a grunt the brave went back and down. Tom kicked out wildly, knowing that his boots were striking his opponent but not where or how seriously. A hand tightened about one ankle and Tom was hauled off balance. He struck the ground with elbow and buttock and heel and the wind was driven out of him. The Apache's knife glinted and drove for his throat. Tom swivelled outside the lunging blade and brought his own arm through a sharp curve that sent his crooked elbow into the back of the Indian's forearm. The Apache's arm was numbed. Tom rolled back and grabbed for it, twisting, turning, hauling it up behind the struggling brave's back.

Both men grunted with effort; sweat glistened on their heads and strain showed in their eyes.

Tom levered the arm higher, higher. The Apache screamed and bucked and Tom was cast up but managed to keep his hold. As he fell to the ground, all of his weight set into his two-handed grip, he heard the Indian's arm crack as clearly as a man stepping on a greyed, brittle twig.

The knife slid away to the ground.

Red-shirt's right arm hung useless and bent.

Tom wiped his hand across his forehead and his eyes, clearing the smarting sweat and dust. When he could see clearly once more he saw that the Apache was moving towards his pistol.

Tom sprang up and ran, wordless rage loud on his lips. He drove his left knee into the crouching Indian's jaw and the sound was like that when he had broken his arm, but hollower, somehow louder. Tom's fingers scooped the gun awkwardly from the ground and his thumb fumbled with the hammer.

He couldn't remember whether there were any shells remaining in the chamber.

Tom's chest was on fire. He felt without looking; looked: the front of his shirt was wet with blood, matted against his chest hair, stuck to his skin. Blood and sweat. Blood. Tom's hand touched the centre of the fire and he winced and his eyes closed.

They didn't open.

Seconds.

Sound forced the eyelids up.

Red-shirt was close upon him, that arm still hanging, bent, like a careless child's discarded toy. The hate in the Indian's eyes drove into his own, sharper even than the blade of his knife. Tom's finger no longer seemed connected to him; just something which lay against the trigger of the gun. Bullets. No bullets. He smelt the stink of the Apache's body and breath and jabbed the barrel of the pistol upwards and his finger, for some reason of its own, squeezed back against the guard.

The explosion welded the two men together.

Tom felt the Apache shudder against him but by now his own eyes were closed fast and he didn't think they would reopen.

They fell together and the sun beat down.

For seconds – minutes – Tom Lenegan's mind struggled to retain consciousness. He was aware of the grease of the Apache's hair and body and the smell of blood and excrement and several times the Indian's hard form shuddered against him.

Tom stopped struggling: the first black bird glistened down through the air.

In his dream Katie's arm wound around his neck and held him close. She was crying. Her tears ran on to his chest and his shirt was wet with them. Tom told her to stop crying – in his dream. He pressed his body against her.

He gradually came to and when he did he saw the Apache. For what seemed longer than the seconds it was, he could not remember what had happened. Only Katie and then he knew that had been a dream. He slid, slowly, from under the Apache's left arm and it fell lifeless to the ground. A spiral of dust rose up and Tom coughed. Christ! The coughing tore his chest apart!

He looked down and then he did remember. All of it. He wanted to prise the shirt away and see how deep the wound was. The flap of wings distracted him. He turned his head and saw half a dozen birds of prey in an ungainly manoeuvre around the dead Indian pony. Further off, two birds sat on top of one of the Apaches, ugly heads dipping, rising, dipping, rising. Every few moments one or other of the birds would flap its wings and lift off into the air, circle and return.

The rage and hatred he had seen on the Indian's face was still there in death; lines carved into a mask, only the eyes might once have been real.

Tom felt his head going forward and he knew that he must stop it. He pushed down with his hands and tried to straighten his arms. Flap of wings. Only in the act of waking did he realize that he'd lost consciousness again. He had no idea for how long. The sun was as strong; still high in the sky. Tom tried to get to his hands and knees and his thigh sang out and immediately he dropped back to the ground and rolled over on to his back. His eyes swam. Tom turned on to his stomach. No! On to his back, head lolling. He blinked. Through a stubborn haze shapes moved off the desert horizon and separated out. Men and horses. Tom's pulse quickened. He tried to count: one . . . two . . . three . . . four . . . five . . . his eyes flickered and shut. Mouth open, his head dropped sideways on to the dust.

Chapter Two

Jed Herne reined in the gelding he was riding and unlooped the canteen from the pommel of his saddle. He unstoppered it and set the round lip of the canteen to his mouth. The water was warm and brackish but at least it broke his thirst. Nothing much else was likely to do that this side of Tucson.

Jed's eyes scanned the terrain. A reddish-grey jumble of rock that was scattered with grey-green brush and occasional flowers which bloomed the brightest of yellows, blues and whites. Ahead the canyon trail went down steeply and levelled out more than four hundred feet below. It twisted, snake-like, between steep enclosing sides before disappearing from sight.

Herne knew what followed.

He knew the trail climbed more slowly until it shifted westward across the last range of hills before the desert. The San Pedro river was behind him and the streams and creeks that ran in profusion down from the high land to the north were more scattered here. Few and drying.

Herne unknotted his bandanna and set the canteen against it, tipping the canteen so that water ran out into the brown cotton without being wasted. He stoppered the canteen and hung it back over the pommel; wiped the bandanna across his forehead and his eyes, then tied it back about his neck.

He knew the territory right enough. He'd lived in it for three years. Three years almost to the day. And that was over three years ago and he'd not ridden back this way since. Didn't think he ever would. Yet something inside had driven him, made him make his way back to this section of southern Arizona like he knew in his gut that if he didn't do it then he'd never be able to live with himself deep inside.

. . . *following the trail of footprints round the side of the cabin through the frozen mud.*

Herne's mind locked the memory back out. He wasn't ready for it. Not yet. The night he'd come back from Tucson with supplies. So close to the third anniversary of his wedding to Louise.

Towards the barn.

'No!'

The gelding lifted its head, startled at the sudden shout. Herne breathed air deep, surprised himself that he should have called aloud. He flicked the reins and set the horse in motion down the trail into the canyon. He watched the sides and left the gelding to watch the path. They'd told him at Fort Grant that two bands of Apaches had jumped the reservation and were causing havoc over an area bordered by Wharton City to the north-west and San Pedro to the south-east. One bunch of them had been rumoured within a dozen miles of Tucson.

Herne wasn't the kind of man to take chances. Not riding into a canyon like this. Not anywhere. That was how he'd lived to the wrong side of forty.

He sat tall in the saddle, an inch and a half over six foot. He weighed a few pounds above two hundred and his shoulders testified to the fact that aging on the frontier had robbed him of neither his suppleness nor strength. Maybe there were a few things he couldn't do as well as he could fifteen, even ten years earlier, but that was the same for all men. The experience he'd accumulated more than made up for that.

Besides, Herne reckoned he could still slug it out with the roughest round-house brawler he'd likely meet up with in a saloon. He could ride day and night without sleep if he had to. Most important, neither eye nor hand had failed him. If it was necessary he could pull that Colt .45 from its greased holster quicker than anyone he'd had to face: and that meant the quickest all across the south and the mid-west. Montana to the Mexican border and beyond.

Herne's hair hung long, touching his dark green wool shirt past the collar. It was lank and black, greying at the temples – greying more every season that came and went. And the rest of his hair too was flecked through with grey. Even the stubble of his beard, three days unshaven, was freckled with it.

Herne clicked his tongue against the roof of his mouth and the gelding responded to that and a slight increase in the pressure of Herne's knees. The horse trotted down the track, Herne looking high, left and right, left and . . .

'Whoa!'

He hauled in on the rein with his left hand, right going across to the smooth stock of the single-shot .55 Sharps that he always carried as a saddle gun.

There was a movement between sections of rough reddish rock, barely discernible yet . . . he shaded his eyes from the sun with a scooped hand and waited. Yes, again. The slightest of signs but he was sure.

Herne drew the Sharps and waited, the curved end of the stock set against his shoulder, eye squinting along the long barrel. Herne's finger was easy on the trigger. He was relaxed, no way tense. The movement came and the finger began to squeeze back.

Herne shifted the rifle away from his body and laughed so that the gelding again looked round, bemused.

It was a wild bear, browny-black, moving slowly along a narrow crevice of rock. Herne watched the animal for several moments before sliding the Sharps back into its scabbard and setting the gelding in motion once again.

The sky over the crested tops of the hills was pale blue with white clouds, flat and narrow, stranded across it. There was little wind and the sun's heat oppressive. Lower down the canyon the shadow of the jagged sides provided some shelter and Herne removed his stained, curved-brim stetson and wiped his fingers around the inside, smearing the sweat away on the leg of his pants. The pants were blue cotton, faded down the front of both legs and one knee worn almost through; his shirt was an uneven red and his hat, originally a light tan, now darkened with grease and fingering and time.

The rest of his belongings were stuffed into the two saddle bags that sat behind him, or rolled inside the slicker that was strapped atop the bags.

Everything he owned – it wasn't much for more than forty years of a life.

Herne looked round as a lone bird swept down the canyon, gliding along on the dipping current of air and then soaring away.

Not much more, Herne thought to himself, than that old bear up there. Not much to show except that I'm still alive while so many . . . so many I knew are nothing more than mounds of earth pushing up from so many hillside cemeteries all over the frontier.

The door stood open, and a light wind had sprung up, making it creak on its hinges. He paused at the entrance, turning and looking round at the land about their spread, knowing that he was seeing it for the last time with that special vision that his wife had brought him.

There had been a time when Jed Herne had had more than the few things he carried with him from settlement to settlement, from town to town and ferry crossing to watering hole. Almost three whole years in which he had had a wife and land and a place he'd built with his own two hands. Almost three years. Almost, for Louise and himself, a child.

Almost.

Hell, thought Herne. I'd as leif it was never as almost!

As soon as the thought crossed his mind, Jed Herne knew that it wasn't true. He wanted nothing to take those three years from him. All he wanted to be rid of was the way of their ending.

The rising sun glistened off the slopes of white, making his eyes hurt.

Herne set one hand to his face to wipe away the lines of sweat that were running from his forehead down either side of his nose and towards his mouth. He blinked away the sweat about his eyes and doing that he almost missed the movement ahead on the trail. A sudden blur from right to left that made Herne blink again and reach once more for the Sharps.

He had no clear idea what it had been. Certainly nothing as bulky and cumbersome as another bear. Bigger than a coyote. A white-tailed deer? An Apache?

Herne waited for minutes, listening acutely, watching.

Nothing.

Gently he touched his spurs to the gelding's flanks and went forward, down on the canyon bed now and the sides picking up the sound of his mount's hoofs and echoing them from side to side until they faded finally upwards into the warm air.

For fifteen minutes Herne made slow progress through the canyon and at the far side he reined in, stood in the stirrups and swivelled round. Rock upon rock, harsh scrub and pieces of whitish stone that reflected the sun. Nothing stirred, least of all now the wind.

Jed Herne unfastened his canteen from the saddle and swallowed a mouthful of the warm water. He hesitated, then swung down to the ground. He removed his stetson and upturned it in his left hand, tipping the canteen over it until water covered the bottom and then some more. Quickly he set the canteen down and held the hat under the gelding's head. The animal drank quickly, greedily, and when it was all gone looked at Herne for more. There was no more – not then.

Herne put the wet hat back on his head and got back up

into the saddle. Still nothing moved, neither in front nor behind. He began to climb the gradual slope out of the canyon.

It had taken Cyrus Clayton more than words to get his daughter to talk. As he had wielded the strap he had told himself that had he done so more often in the past few years then the present trouble would have been avoided. But bringing up a daughter without a woman in the house was not an easy task for a man with a ranch to run and four sons to raise, so perhaps Katie had suffered from neglect.

He did not neglect her then.

Only when she was sobbing so that it sounded as if she must choke on her own tears, did Cyrus lay the strap aside. And then she had told him what he wanted to know – what he had already more or less guessed but wanted to hear from his daughter's own lips.

The name of Tom Lenegan.

Cyrus Clayton had gone to fetch his sons: Hal, Jack, Stewart and John. Horses and rifles. Ammunition. Water and supplies. Rope. He wasn't sure how far Tom Lenegan would have got, nor if he would try to run when he got wind that the Claytons were after him.

But, whatever he did, old Cyrus was determined to catch him and mete out the proper justice. Young tearaways with little prospect of ever amounting to anything did not go courting his daughter without his permission and get away with it. A lesson had to be taught here. To Katie as well as to anyone else who might consider his pretty young daughter easy pickings.

Seventeen.

Cyrus Clayton hawked a ball of phlegm into his mouth and turned his head to one side and spat. He had never guessed that picking up the Lenegan boy's trail would be so easy – nor that when they found him it would be as it was.

They rode in until they were sure of what they saw. Cyrus was never a tall man and now that he was tending towards fat he looked almost squat. His face was round, with a small mouth which grew a meagre moustache along its upper lip – both mouth and moustache looking adrift. His dark hair was cut short and mostly hidden beneath the peaked stetson that he mostly wore.

All of his sons had inherited their father's stocky body and roundness of face; all except the youngest, John. He was the only one who resembled his mother. Lean, thin, high cheekbones and skin that was fair even after the hottest sun. The youngster's hair had been close to pure white when a kid; now it was the colour of ripening corn. His father's affections for him varied between an irrational loving and a hatred that was so intense that Cyrus wanted to strike him from his sight. Both because of the way in which John reminded Cyrus of his wife.

'That's him, all right, Pa,' called Hal, wiping the sleeve of his plaid shirt along one side of his jaw. 'That's Lenegan.'

Cyrus nodded and pulled out his saddle gun and levered a shell into the chamber.

'You think there's more Apache around, Pa?' asked Jack.

Cyrus looked at him as though he were a fool. 'I do not.'

'That for Lenegan?' asked Stewart, patting the neck of the black mare he was astride.

'Could be we're too late for that,' cut in Hal. 'Looks like them Apache did for him first.'

'Tom Lenegan really see to all them Indians by hisself, Pa?' asked Stewart. 'Don't see how he could have done that.'

'Me neither,' agreed Jack.

Cyrus spat and the yellow-green ball rolled a few inches through the dust until it was choked to a stop. 'Best we stop chawin' and get to him an' see. But keep your eyes skinned. I ain't trusting nothin' here till we get a better look.'

The birds of prey rose up reluctantly with slow,

half-sated flapping of wings. The Claytons went from one Apache to another, shaking their heads in wonder. All save Cyrus – he rode direct to Tom Lenegan and pointed his rifle down at him and waited for the least sign of movement. He was still waiting when his sons gathered round.

'He dead, Pa?'

'Sure he's dead.'

'An' no good riddance.'

Cyrus pointed to his eldest son. 'Get down there.'

'Huh?'

'Get down an' see if he's breathin'.'

Hal climbed from the saddle and went, bow-legged, to where Tom Lenegan was on his back, close by the red-shirted Apache whose guts were half-spilled out, half torn away by some bird's bloodied beak.

'Jesus, Pa! It stinks down here like . . .'

'Just get it done.' There was a finality in his father's voice that didn't encourage delay.

Hal held his head above Tom's chest, trying to make sure that his face didn't touch the blood-soaked shirt. He couldn't register anything at all.

'Don't know, Pa, but . . .'

'What the hell's the use of not knowing, boy? Make certain. I sure don't want to have ridden all this way for nothin'. To have got beat to it by a bunch of savages.'

The slightest trace of breath issued from Tom Lenegan's nostrils and from the slimmest of cracks between his lips. Only by resting his own face on Tom's could Hal be positive. He stood up and brushed his hands down the sides of his pants.

'Well?'

'He's breathin', Pa. Certain.'

Cyrus Clayton smiled. 'Let's get him out of this sun.'

They laid Tom Lenegan back against rough red rock and left him there while they drank from their canteens and the youngest saw to the horses. Once a noise came from Tom's mouth and all five turned fast towards him, but his eyes were still closed and the only movement they saw was a slow opening and closing of the fingers of his right hand.

'All right,' said Cyrus, his thirst quenched. 'Let's get to it.'

He threw water in Tom Lenegan's face and reached forward and slapped him hard, one side and then the other.

Nothing happened.

Cyrus repeated the process, the knuckles of his hand driving Tom's face hard against the rock.

'Pa . . .' John began but got no further as his father whirled round to face him.

'S'matter, boy? You don't like what I'm doin'?'

'I . . .'

Cyrus spat into the space between them. 'Damn, boy, I don't know how I managed to get you at the end of a line of men. I swear I don't. You got the spine of a jackass wearin' a taffeta party dress, an' that's the truth.'

Hal hollered with laughter; the others made no response. John's face became paler and his left eye twitched shut as if it had been his cheek his father had been slapping against the rock.

Cyrus took a step towards his youngest son. 'You know what this trash has been doin', don't you?'

John nodded.

'You know why we're here? What we got to do this for?'

Cyrus's eyes blazed in his head, protruding from their sockets.

'Think on your sister and get them cowardly ways out of your head for good an' all!'

John tried to hold his father's gaze but he couldn't; his eyes turned away and although he was no longer looking he was still aware of the disgust in his father's eyes.

Tom Lenegan moved his right arm downwards a little and groaned.

'Pa!'

Cyrus glowered at his youngest boy a second or two

longer and then went back to Lenegan.

'He's comin' to, Pa,' said Stewart, excitement rising in his voice.

Cyrus pointed at Hal. 'Let him have some more of that water.'

The contents of the canteen washed over Tom's face and he jerked his head suddenly forward and shook it from side to side, eyes finally blinking open. He saw men standing before him but they failed to register clearly. Shapes that were roughly the shapes of men and nothing more. His eyes closed and his head slumped back.

'Again!' shouted Cyrus.

This time Tom recognized who the men were. He wished that he didn't. He thought of Katie and as he was thinking of her Cyrus grabbed him by the arms and stood him off the rock.

'I'm glad you're still livin', Lenegan. I'm glad them bastards didn't finish you off out there.'

Tom's mind was trying to work, trying to think clearly, anxious to find some way of explaining, of attempting to make it all right.

'Katie,' he said, and Cyrus's fist drove into the side of his face.

Tom rocked back on to the rock and one of his legs went under him. Pain surged up from his thigh and tightened hard across his chest. His eyes closed and he didn't want to open them again.

He did open them.

Cyrus Clayton's face was thrust up close to his own and he could smell the sourness and contempt on the man's breath.

'Don't ever let me hear you speak her name again.'

Tom gulped in air and even that hurt.

He said, quietly and slowly, 'Is she all right?'

'That's good, coming from you,' sneered Cyrus.

'I mean . . . I meant . . . the Apache.'

Cyrus stepped back. 'She ain't none of your concern.'

'No, I . . .'

'Not no more.'

Tom looked from one to another of the brothers – only John refused to meet his eyes.

'Get that rope,' Cyrus said to Jack. 'Hal an' Stewart, hold his arms.'

Tom tried to struggle but they held him fast. Cyrus set his fingers against the front of Tom's shirt and laughed; then he ripped it back hard, both arms moving outwards. The cotton tore away from the skin, taking scabbed blood with it, breaking the wound open fresh.

'Jesus, Pa!' shouted John, moving towards his father. 'You can't!'

Cyrus swung his right arm so that the back of his hand struck his son in the side of the neck. John staggered back and fell to his knees, clutching his throat and gasping for breath.

After a moment's hesitation, Jack started to go to him, but a look from his father stopped him short.

Blood was running from the knife wound in Tom Lenegan's chest.

'I'm teachin' you a lesson,' said Cyrus Clayton. 'One you ain't about to forget. Supposin' you live to remember anythin'. Either way, you won't come near my girl again. You won't see her an' you won't speak to her an' if you try I'll shoot you down in the street like the cheap trash you are.'

He nodded to his sons. 'Turn him.'

They laid Tom face forward on the rock, ropes to his wrists held taut so that he could scarcely struggle at all. Cyrus took a second rope, a length of stout hemp, the end knotted and tied fast. He swung some three feet of the rope end through the air, a grim smile coming to his small mouth.

'You remember what this is for, Lenegan. You remember good.'

The rope hit Tom first on the right shoulder blade and

drove his chest into the roughness of the rock and Tom screamed loud.

'Hear that?' asked Cyrus in triumph. 'Hear that cowardly bastard yell?'

The second blow was low and hit him in the kidneys and his legs would have buckled beneath him had not the ropes prevented it from happening. The third blow struck his spine and Tom's head jerked upwards and his chin grazed open.

The fourth blow was never delivered.

The .45 slug whined off the rock a couple of feet high over Tom's head and went ricochetting into the distance. Cyrus let the rope trail and turned fast. Hal Clayton turned faster, letting go of his own rope as his hand moved towards his holster.

'Don't do it, son,' said Herne. His thumb had already brought back the hammer of the Colt and now he covered Hal's move. Hal didn't hesitate long; his hand rested on the air and then fell to his side.

'Who the hell are you?' shouted Cyrus, anger in his eyes and voice. 'Bustin' in here like this.'

'Who I am don't matter,' said Herne. 'Let's just say I don't take too kind to five men gangin' up on one man who's already wounded bad.'

'That ain't none of your damn business!'

Herne grinned and nodded towards the Colt. 'While I'm holdin' this it is.'

Cyrus glanced round at his sons, uncertain of what to do. 'I'm warnin' you, stranger,' he blustered. 'You don't know who you're dealin' with. Now you ride on and mind your own business an' we'll forget this ever happened.'

Herne nodded, looked at Tom, whose body had slumped down the rock towards the ground.

'What'd he do?'

'That ain't none of your concern. Now . . .'

'Rustle your cattle? Steal your money? What?'

John Clayton said, not looking up at Herne as he spoke, not looking at any of them: 'He went courting my sister.'

'That's all?'

'That's all,' said John.

'You shut your mouth!' shouted Cyrus, clenching his fists.

John did as he was told, looked away and began to walk slowly towards the horses. Stewart and Jack hesitated; Hal was still in two minds about making a play for the pistol at his side. Cyrus Clayton was shaking with impotent rage, helpless under the stranger's gun.

'Who the . . . who in hell's name are you?'

'Jed Herne.'

'Herne?'

'Uh-huh.'

Hal ventured a pace forward, his right arm starting to fan out. 'Pa, he's nobody. Just a bum who happened along. I mean look at him, just look at him. Whatever he might have been once, he ain't nothin' now.' The arm spread wider. 'Nothin'.'

Cyrus hesitated, Herne's name turning in his mind . . . somewhere, down on the border, maybe, some town or other he'd passed through perhaps ten years past he'd heard that name. Herne. Something like it. Not just plain Herne and not Jed Herne, the way he'd announced himself then. No, it was . . .

'Pa, I tell you, he's a washed-up bum. A down-an'-out. Nothin'.'

Herne the . . . Herne the . . . Cyrus' mind raced as he clenched the nails of his fingers tight into his hand and sweat pumped from the pores of his body.

'Pa.'

Behind them, Tom Lenegan's body made a final pitch to the ground. The sound drew Herne's attention, his eyes flickered away and Hal saw his chance. Seized it. Seized the gun at his hip and rocked his body back as the gun came up, the hammer moving smoothly back as it swung through the angle, a smile bordering on the older son's mouth – easy, easy, easy: nothing but an old tramp – finger tightening on the trigger.

'Herne the Hunter!' the name leapt aloud from Cyrus' lips as the memory shot home.

Herne put a bullet through Hal Clayton's chest, splitting the breast bone, driving him back, feet jolted clear of the ground. The bullet deflected sideways and down, exiting with a burst of tissue and blood and fragmented bone a few inches above the left hip.

Hal's gun was tossed into the air and a gout of blood flew from his mouth as his back struck rock.

'No!'

Herne's legs were spaced for balance, left arm angled outwards for the same purpose; the Colt was ready again and the narrowed eyes above it showed their intent.

Hal's legs kicked up viciously and his back arched through an unnatural curve. Stewart and Jack knelt on either side of him, hands trying to quell both the movement and the pain.

His father was still staring at the gun in Herne's hand, then at his lined, weathered face. 'Herne the Hunter,' he said in a voice soft enough for church. 'I thought you were dead.'

Herne nodded down towards the bent form of Clayton's son. 'I ain't the one who's dead.'

Cyrus Clayton closed his eyes and hung his head and his youngest son went and stood beside him, wanting to put a hand on his father's shoulder, wanting to offer him comfort yet not knowing how.

Chapter Three

The room was on the upper floor at the back of the house. The walls had been painted white, the simple chair and small table and the dressing-stand painted white also. Above the bed hung a sampler in which the words, Bless This House, had been worked in red on a blue and gold background. For all that those colours had begun to fade, they presented almost the only brightness in the room.

A brown blanket lay over the bed and Tom Lenegan sat propped against off-white pillows, a tray resting on his legs. It was the fifth day he had eaten broth and though it was as good as it had been on the first, he was plain tired of it. Tired of laying in bed and being told to rest. Tired of the ache in his chest and leg whenever he did attempt to move. More than tired of not seeing Katie, of not knowing what had happened to her since the day he had been wounded and beaten. Since the day her eldest brother had been killed by Herne the Hunter.

Herne had seemed too big for the room when he stepped inside, his shoulders were forced to stoop by the low ceiling and his head to bend. He had been over to visit with Tom several times since getting him to Tucson; he'd got to like the youngster, admire him for the straight way in which he saw things. He sympathized with him in his feelings for Clayton's daughter and tended to take his side – especially after what he'd seen the old man trying to do to Tom with that rope end.

Herne had even ridden out to the small ranch run by Lenegan's folks and told them what had happened, reassured them that everything was going to be all right. Their boy would mend with time and mend good.

Gus Lenegan was taller than Herne by a good inch and

he was as thin as a larch branch. A long neck and a small head perched on top of it as if a strong wind might blow it off. But the eyes that moved in the head were bright and lively and the mouth was anything but mean. The hand that gripped Herne's was strong, too, but it was the left instead of the right. Gus Lenegan's right sleeve was tied and knotted midway between his shoulder and where the elbow would have been. He'd had a bad accident with a steer a few years back, the thing had festered, gangrene had set in. It was only by amputating that the doctor had saved Gus's life.

Gus had been grateful and carried on best as he could. But there were things he could no longer do.

'Should've been me,' he'd said to Herne as they sat out on the small planked porch. 'Me out lookin' for him, helpin' him. Not a stranger. Me.'

'Gus,' said his wife, Martha, sitting forward in her chair, an old weathered rocker that stayed out rain or shine, 'don't talk that way. Mister Herne here'll think we're ungrateful for what he done.'

'No, ma'am, I . . .'

'Call me Martha, won't you?'

'Sure, Martha, I reckon I know what . . . what Gus means an' I don't take no offence.' He looked at Gus. 'You wasn't to know he was in any trouble anyway, I guess.'

'That's true, Gus,' said Martha Lenegan. 'There was no way of us knowing about any of it. The Apaches, them Claytons, none of it. We brung up Tom to stand on his own feet and go where he wants to without havin' to ask a bye your leave from us. We brung him up like that an' I . . .' She broke off and turned her head aside for a moment, as if a mote of dust had caught in an eye corner. 'I reckon we done a good job an' we can be proud. Real proud.'

She stood up sharply, a small woman with tight dark hair and wiry arms, hands that were veined and strong and which she now clenched in front of her apron.

'There,' she said, 'now let that be an end to all your mawkish talk, Gus Lenegan. I've had tea on the brew since Mi . . . since Jed here arrived and there's a fruit cake I'm unwrapping so we'll settle into those before Jed rides back to town.'

She looked at the two men as if daring either of them to disagree. When neither did, she nodded quickly, like a bird pecking food, and went into the house.

The men sat for a while in silence. Behind them the sun was mellowing to a deep orange, the shadows of trees lengthening down the sides of the valley. Smoke rose up from the chimney stack and drifted towards the south-west.

'You got a fine woman there,' said Herne, looking in the direction of the open door.

'Yeah,' Gus Lenegan nodded. 'No man could've had finer. No man could've had a better life with a woman than I've had. That's a fact.' He prodded his pipe towards Herne and a smile shone in his eyes. 'Tell you somethin' I ain't told many folk ever.'

'Go on.'

'First time I saw Martha, it was a little over half-hour afore we was due to be wed.'

Herne started to say something and then waited; now that Gus had started he reasoned the man would explain in his own way.

'Stage was late on its run, some trouble changing horses at one of the way stations, some fool thing like that. Martha nearly missed it altogether.' He chuckled. 'There'd've been hell to pay, then. Preacher'd wanted payin' just the same, folks who'd brought food an' drink wouldn't've known whether to take it back and try with it the next day or get it down 'em on the spot.'

The chuckle grew to an outright laugh.

'I was all dressed up in a suit I'd hired from the store just for the afternoon an' hoppin' around in it like a rooster who's got hisself all spruced up but can't get into the henhouse.'

Gus laughed and shook his head and then struck a match and relit his pipe.

'I set me an advert in this paper. *Santa Fe Star.* "Young man with good land and prospects wants wife. Must be young and strong and like hard work." Got three replies. Two of 'em sent drawin's of themselves they'd got done special, just so's to show how pretty they was. An' – ' he wiped his hand down his leg and gave his knee a scratch – 'they was – if them pictures were true. Martha, though, she didn't send no picture. She wasn't interested in seemin' pretty; she wrote with a good strong hand – wrote it herself, too, I found that out soon enough – an' told me how she was used to workin' from sun-up to sun-down an' how she was livin' with her folks but wanted to get off on her own on account of how the land they had wasn't enough to support the lot of 'em. Twelve kids in Martha's family an' her the third eldest. Nineteen she was. Nineteen an' three weeks that time she wrote.'

Gus drew on his pipe and leaned back. The sun was deeper and darker and seemed to fill the valley-end; the wind was keening towards cold.

'Knew right off she was the one I wanted. Got a friend to write back and tell her to catch the next stage she could an' to let me know when she was comin' so's I could rustle up the preacher an' all.' He smiled, remembering. 'She was late but soon as she stepped down off that coach I knew I'd done the right thing an' I ain't never for one minute regretted it.'

'You two intending to sit out here till it gets dark,' said Martha, standing in the doorway, 'or are you coming in for this tea now?'

She gave no indication of how long she'd been standing there listening, save for a look of satisfaction and pride when Herne walked past her and into the house.

The cake was rich and moist and the tea black and strong. The house was simply furnished, mostly with things

Gus had made himself when he still had two hands to do it with. Herne sat there quietly drinking his tea and thinking they were good people and that Tom had been fortunate to have been born to parents like them. He wondered why they had never had any other children – or perhaps they had and no others had survived.

A cloud passed across his eyes and a wedge of pain forced itself into his brain.

'Jed?' Martha sat forward. 'Somethin' wrong?'

Herne held up his hand, palm outwards. 'Nothin',' he said, and she let it drop.

'Was you ever married?' asked Gus just a few moments later, one half of his mouth filled with cake.

Herne nodded. 'One time.'

Inside, it was very quiet. She had . . .

Gus coughed a few crumbs from his mouth and wiped the side of his hand across it; he was leaning forward across the table, waiting for Herne to say more, but Herne had said all he wanted.

Martha Lenegan knew it, even if her husband didn't.

She stood up with the knife in her hand and bent over the cake. ' 'Nother piece, Jed?'

'No, thanks, ma'am. Sorry, Martha. I ate all I could. It was good, though, and I thank you for it. Sooner Tom gets home the better, seems to me. You can fatten him up an' get him back strong better'n most.'

Martha smiled and nodded. Herne stood up.

'Sure you don't want to stay the night?' asked Gus. 'We can break open a bottle, play some checkers. Talk.'

'No, thanks. Some other time, maybe.'

He reached across the table and clasped Gus's hand. On an impulse, as he passed her, Martha caught hold of Herne's arm, lifted up her face and kissed him on the cheek.

'Thanks for what you did for Tom, Jed. We won't forget it. None of us.'

Herne waved and stepped outside. He untied his horse

from the corral fence and climbed into the saddle. He'd be back in Tucson before the night was full dark.

When next he saw Tom, the youngster was sitting up and taking a lot more notice. His cheeks showed some colour and as soon as Herne came into the room he called out excitedly, 'I heard from her. From Katie.'

'You did? That's fine. But how?'

'She sent me a note. Yesterday.'

'How did she manage that?'

Tom shook his head. 'I ain't sure exactly. There's a couple of hands work out at the spread an' I guess she got one of them to bring it in when he come to town. Anyway, that don't matter.'

'She okay?' Herne asked, sitting on the end of the bed.

'Her father's keepin' her more or less a prisoner since he got back. Won't let her out of the house. One of the brothers goes with her whenever she does.'

'You still seem to be smilin',' said Herne. 'How's that?'

Tom flushed a little. 'Says she wants to marry me more than ever. Can't wait to get away. She's sad about her brother, about Hal, right enough. I mean, they was close kin, but that ain't changed anything either.'

Herne wondered if it would have had Tom killed Hal and not himself. He kept the thought quiet and waited for Tom to carry on.

'She's going to run off.'

'How can she if she's watched all the time?'

Tom smiled. 'She'll wait till John's the one lookin' to her. He's the youngest an' he don't hold with what his pa says, what he does. The way he treats Katie like she ain't got no mind of her own. When she's with him, she'll get a horse and ride out to my folk's place.'

'Don't you reckon,' asked Herne, 'that'll be bringin' your folks a parcel of trouble?'

'How come?'

''Cause if she runs off, Cyrus is goin' to hear 'bout it

afore long and he's not going to be in any two minds 'bout where to start lookin'.'

Tom sat forward, wincing slightly with the movement. 'Don't worry 'bout that. We'll get married right off and there won't be anything Clayton can do about it. Once we're man and wife he'll have to accept it.'

Herne couldn't see that had to be the case at all; the expression on his face told Tom so.

'Well, what else are we supposed to do? If I wait for Clayton to consent, I'll be waitin' till either I'm dead or he is.'

'Then maybe you should marry the girl and take off for somewhere he can't find you.'

'Run, you mean?'

Herne hesitated. 'Sort of, I guess.'

'I ain't runnin'. That's for certain.'

Herne stood up, he turned away from the bed, went to the window and glanced down to the street, looked back at Tom once more. 'What happens if you two stick an' Clayton and his sons come after you? Your pa'll feel he's got to side with you even though he ain't got but one arm to do it with. You'll face up to the girl's kin and then what happens if you come through? How's she goin' to feel if she's seen you gun down her brothers, maybe her pa?'

Tom avoided Herne's stare. 'She loves me,' he said to the far wall.

'Ever occur to you she might love them as well?'

'The way they treat her?' Tom blazed.

'Sure. Takes an awful lot to stop folks lovin' their kin. One hell of a lot.'

Tom turned away again. 'That may be. All I know is she loves me more.'

'All right. But you think on what I said about bringin' trouble on your own ma and pa.' He pointed a finger at Tom's face. 'You give that some careful thought. You hear?'

Tom nodded, almost imperceptibly, but he said nothing

more. Herne shrugged and walked away, leaving the youngster to his own thoughts.

His own thoughts. Herne went from saloon to saloon, talking to men at the bars, sitting in at five card draw or stud, drinking beer and whisky and doing anything that would put off the time when he was going to be alone for the remainder of the night. That night. He knew his mind had gone so far along the line that it was impossible to draw back now.

Out in the street with the sound of laughter still coming from the open windows and the batwing doors of saloons, with horses still tethered to hitching rails and men wandering aimlessly along, Herne stood absolutely still. He stared up at the fullness of the moon and felt a cold wind race through him as he saw its whiteness.

The rising sun glistened off the slopes of white, making his eyes hurt.

He took half a dozen paces north in the direction of the whorehouse, reasoning that a night bought there would keep it – keep her – from his mind. Almost as quickly as the idea came to him, he dismissed it. He wasn't going to be able to forget Louise in the arms of a whore, no matter how beautiful or attentive she might be. He never had and he never would. Tonight, more than ever, it would be useless to try. Too much had happened to shut her out.

Herne walked back on to the boardwalk, pushed back one section of the doors and went in amongst the smoke and noise. He paid over the counter for a bottle of best whisky and stuffed that down into his coat pocket. Then he went back to his hotel room.

He took the bottle from his pocket and sat it on the floor near the head of the bed, he hung his coat over the brass bed rail and sat down to pull off his boots. Herne unstoppered the bottle and set it to his lips. He drank in short swallows, letting the whisky hit the back of his throat and burn a little before taking more. The sounds of the Tucson night drifted around him and merged into something unidentifiable: he forgot about them. He put the bottle back on the floor.

He remembered.

The room was still and quiet. He lay there for a moment, on his back, trying to come to terms with the new day. Then he realized that there was a sound missing that should have been there. He couldn't hear the breathing of his wife.

Quickly he stretched out a hand, but the sheets were as cold as death, all the way clear across to the other side. He flung back the blankets, and the white expanse of the bed lay open before him, like a new land viewed from the peak of a high range of mountains.

They were white and pure, except where Louise had lain.

There the white was dappled and clotted with brown.

Dark brown that was still red in places where the blood hadn't quite dried.

He was out of bed and into his trousers, padding in bare feet across the room, easing the door open to the rest of the cabin, glancing around it, and instantly realizing that it too was empty. As he stepped across the floor, his feet touched a patch of something wet and sticky. Something that he hardly needed to touch with his finger to know that it was a small circle of blood, spreading out as though it had fallen from something moving.

On the table, propped up against the coffee pot, there was a sheet of notepaper as white as the sheets in the bedroom. As white as the snow that lay beyond the windows.

And on the sheet, scrawled in his wife's hand, was the single word 'Jed'.

Herne stood quite still and took three deep breaths. When his breathing had steadied, he picked up the flimsy sheet of paper, taking it to the front window, pulling back the curtain, holding the letter so that the pale light fell across it.

'Dearest Jed,' it began. 'By the time you read this, I will be gone. What happened last night is too much for me

ever to forget, and whatever you might think, it will always lie between us. What they did has killed everything. I was going to have another baby. Doc Newman reckoned that after last time it would be my last chance. But I know from the bleeding that they killed it. I wanted to have your son, my dear heart. Now I can't give it to you, so there isn't much point in anything. Help look after Becky, as I do not think that Bill is much good with her. Please believe that I have always loved you, my darling, and that you brought me happiness like I never thought I would see. What a pity it is that our time has been so short, but that is God's will, and we must abide it. Well, darling, time is getting on, and I have things to do. The dress is lovely and will do for the funeral. Thank you for it. You always were thoughtful to me, Jed. Again, my dear, I am so sorry that all must end this way. Goodbye for ever, until we meet again beyond. Your dearest Louise.'

The writing was small and neat and Jed found some of it hard to decipher, tilting the paper to try and strain more light on to it. When he'd finished, he went out through the open front door, following the trail of footprints round the side of the cabin through the frozen mud.

Towards the barn.

The door stood open, and a light wind had sprung up, making it creak on its hinges. He paused at the entrance, turning and looking round at the land about their spread, knowing that he was seeing it for the last time with that special vision that his wife had brought him. The rising sun glistened off the slopes of white, making his eyes hurt.

Inside, it was very quiet. She had climbed up on a box to do it and then merely stepped silently into eternity. The noose had dug into her neck, leaving an ugly burn, but apart from that she looked very peaceful, hands hanging limply at her sides, a shaft of light gleaming off the gold wedding ring.

And the dress looked pretty. Dark green velvet, with

white lace at collar and cuffs. Direct from Paris, France, like the book said.

It was a very pretty dress.

His wife had said it: the pity of their time being so short. Three years out of a lifetime – two lifetimes, his much longer than hers. And it had been cut short by seven men. Seven men who had tramped across the open land from the carriage of their snow-bound train, already drunk and rowdy and ripe for trouble. Seven men who had raped her horribly, hatefully. Seven of them.

Herne had tracked them down. With some it had been easy, they had not been able to run too far, they hadn't had sufficient time to cover their tracks. Others had both time and space – and, more important, money. They had not made Herne's task of exacting vengeance easy. In a way that was good: he hadn't wanted it to come easy. It needed to be hard and dangerous and it needed the greater satisfaction that would come after such a hunt.

When all seven men were dead that should have been an end to it.

Should have been.

Herne had learned that no amount of killing would erase the memory of Louise from his mind: no amount of blood would wash away his memory of her racked body or her dismembered mind. A mind left with little save the gentleness that had formed the words of her final letter.

He still knew each word, could see them on the page.

He could conjure up each contour of Louise's face and every fold of her body. Disturbed by dreams that moved through him like clouds scudding the sky, there were fleeting moments when he smelt her breath on his face and was conscious of the perfume of her skin, the soft touch of it on his shoulder. Then he would start awake and shake his head, blink both eyes away from sleep, and reach beside him in the bed.

Exactly as he had that early March morning in '82.

Only this time there was no drying blood, there was no spreading stain of brown and red. If anyone lay there it was a girl he had bought and paid for the night before and whose back was now turned towards him and whose five dollars now lay lightly clenched in the small hand that rested at the edge of the pillow.

At those times Herne would slide from the bed silently, throw water on his face and quickly dress, walking outside into the cold freshness of the morning air.

Not now: Herne sat on the side of the bed and reached down for the bottle but it never came to his mouth. He simply set it back down again and thought about the first time he'd ever clapped eyes on Louise . . .

Chapter Four

It had been the summer of '78 and the Lincoln County Range War had just erupted to a new height of blood-letting. Jed Herne had been trapped in the McSween place, along with Billy Bonney, Charlie Bowdre, the McSweens themselves and nearly a dozen more. Outside there'd been the law Murphy and Dolan had bought to replace Sheriff Bill Brady, who had failed to survive an encounter with Bonney's band of self-styled regulators. It wasn't only the law, either, there was every gun that Murphy and Dolan could buy and press into service.

In and around the McSween place, the fighting had gone on for three days and nights and a lot of men had lost their lives – some of them men whom Herne had been pleased to play a hand of cards with, share a drink or a joke or two.

If a detachment of US Army hadn't showed up they'd likely have stuck at it till there were more of them dead or wounded than anything else.

As it was the Army had dragged them out and some kind of uneasy truce had existed ever since. So, on the first day that Herne rode into Lincoln itself after the McSween shoot-out, he did so with a lot of caution. He wasn't going in alone, of course, nothing as foolhardy as that. Charlie Bowdre went along for the ride, as did a couple of the other boys, and all of them went well-armed and expecting trouble. But, as Jed had said, there wasn't no way they were going to stay skulking around and hiding up for ever. If you did that then it meant that Murphy and Dolan had won a whole lot more than they really had.

They went in early in the morning, the sun angled sharply from the east and striking rooftops and flushing out the red in the adobe walls. Shadows were long and sharply etched.

Herne's eyes kept shifting this way and that, looking out for the first sign of one of the other side's possemen with the black stetsons that they favoured. All he saw was a deputy sitting on a chair outside the sheriff's office with a rifle across his lap and his hands folded over it. The deputy saw the four men come riding down the street and eased his hat brim down so as to get a more shaded look at them. But he never moved his hands nor made any attempt to bring the rifle into play. He even, as Herne and the others rode slowly past, gave them a curt nod before pushing back his hat brim and stretching his legs right out.

Herne didn't like that, either, didn't trust it, but he couldn't think of what to do about it – other than keep the leather thong clear of the hammer of his Colt and keep his eyes skinned.

By the time they reached the eating house that the McSween men favoured, no one who looked like trouble had appeared.

'Don't like it,' said Bowdre, 't'ain't natural.'

Herne turned in his saddle and looked carefully up and down the street. As yet there were few folk about. 'Me neither, Charlie, but what the hell?'

'Yeah, Jed, let's get somethin' hot inside us, anyway.'

The four men tied up their horses to the hitching rail and went inside. Three-quarters of an hour and four plates of ham and eggs and grits later, they stepped back out into strong sunlight. Men were moving with a sense of purpose along both sides of the street, crossing from one boardwalk to the other. A feed wagon was making slow progress towards the livery stable close by the western edge of town. Two scrawny dogs chased one another and yelped and yapped and turned tail and chased in the opposite direction. As they raced between the legs of one of the team drawing the wagon, the horse baulked and tossed its heavy head and the driver cursed and lashed out with his whip.

Herne and Bowdre glanced up and down the street while the other two men untethered the horses.

'Store?' asked Bowdre.

Herne nodded. 'Sure.'

Herne was ducking under the hitching post when he heard a quick scuffle from Bowdre's boots at back of him and a yelled warning from Bowdre's mouth.

He grabbed at the post with his left hand, hauling himself through fast and reaching for the Colt .45 at his hip with the other. His fingers closed about the smooth butt as he heard Bowdre again and saw him pointing out into the street.

Herne slid the Colt up and spun about, following the line of Bowdre's arm.

The feed wagon lurched back into motion and behind it Herne glimpsed a blur of black hat.

'There!' yelled Charlie, his own pistol now in his hand. 'There. Look.'

Herne thumbed the hammer smoothly back and waited – fractions of time only that passed with the slowness of the moon gliding down the sky.

The man showed clear behind the wagon. Tall and thin, walking slow and with a pronounced stoop, the hat on his head black certainly but not the kind of stetson that the possemen wore. This was much broader brimmed, so that the edges folded down in places, its crown was less full and flat at the top. It wasn't a posseman's hat: rather the hat of a preacher. The rest of the man's clothes added to that impression. The suit he wore was also black, fraying at the cuffs and almost worn through at elbows and knees, as if he was a man who did an uncomfortable amount of praying.

'It's okay, Charlie.'

Herne straightened up, releasing the hammer of his Colt and moving the pistol back towards the greased holster.

As he did so, the preacher turned to face, him, turned and stopped, stopped and stared. Even from the opposite side of the street, Herne could read the intensity in the man's eyes, small and dark and like beads of jet in his face. The mouth was small and the lips almost not there, little colour showed on his cheeks. He kept his eyes on Herne and reached into his right-hand pocket. Herne stayed the Colt on its way to the holster. The preacher drew a small black leather-bound book from his pocket and held it out towards Herne as if it were a talisman.

Herne snorted and dropped his Colt into place, swinging on his heel and reaching for the reins of his horse from one of the others.

'Let's get them things,' he said curtly.

Herne put the preacher and his bible from his mind and concentrated on the task at hand. They bought the things they needed, delaying only while Charlie Bowdre deliberated over buying a new pipe, and prepared to head back out of town.

'Ain't we goin' to get us a beer afore we go?' asked one of the men.

Herne and Bowdre exchanged doubtful glances.

'Don't rightly know,' said Charlie hesitantly, 'only it seems . . .'

'Seems what? Hell, I'm only talkin' 'bout gettin' a beer. One miserable little glass of beer.'

'Well . . .'

'Maybe we better not push our luck,' put in Herne.

'Aw, Jed . . .'

Herne shrugged. 'Have it your own way. You want a drink, the two of you, you take it. Me an' Charlie here, I think we'll ride on out. We take it slow, you can catch us up inside an hour.'

Now it was the turn of the other two to exchange doubtful looks.

'Hell, I thought all of us . . .'

Herne shook his head. 'You thought wrong.'

The man sighed. 'Okay. Have it your way. We'll get us a beer some other time.'

'Yeah.'

Bowdre pushed open the door and went out on to the boardwalk. It was hotter and noisier and the air was almost still. Sweat immediately began to run down his neck and from between his arms.

'Jesus,' exclaimed the man behind him. 'We're goin' to burn up.'

'Damned right,' echoed his friend. 'Glass of beer would've come just about right.'

Herne wasn't saying anything. He hadn't even noticed the extra heat. He was looking beyond Charlie Bowdre and the others to where the preacher was standing beside a flat-bedded wagon some few yards into the street. He was standing there and staring up at Herne as if he'd been waiting for him to emerge from the store. A look of more than recognition passed between them. And then Herne's eyes moved on to the seat of the wagon and they saw Louise.

He didn't know then that was her name.

He didn't know anything about her except that she was pretty enough to make him forget the preacher's stare. Herne saw nothing for those moments save the slim beauty of her face, the natural colour of her cheeks set against the milkiness of her skin, the generous width of her mouth, the least tremor of her lower lip.

Her hair was dark, almost black, and curled loosely about her face. She wore a simple gingham dress, blue and white, gathered at the waist. She realized that Herne was looking at her and for several seconds she looked back at him and there was a directness, a candour, about her that struck Herne as different.

But the woman sitting alongside her frowned and bent towards her and said something that Herne could not hear and the girl fussed with her hands and turned her head away.

Herne knew that she was young but not how young.

'Jed.'

He turned at the sound of Charlie's voice.

'You changed your mind 'bout a beer, or what?'

Herne shook his head. 'No, Charlie, I ain't changed my mind.'

Charlie Bowdre shook his head, uncertain, and mounted up. Herne tied the sack of supplies he'd bought to the pommel of his saddle and did the same. The preacher helped first his wife and then his daughter down from the wagon and started off towards the store. Herne had pulled his horse round and was moving out into the wide street. Bowdre's shadow fell across him, like a cloud across his eye. The other pair were already heading down the street, heads turned now to see what was holding Herne and Bowdre back.

None of them saw the shotgun poke over the lower sill of the upstairs window opposite, show itself then quickly angle down.

No one knew of its existence other than the man whose hands held it, slightly nervously, in place and squinted along the length of the barrels.

Other than his colleague who was standing well back down the alley fifteen yards along the street. A third man who was positioned back towards the livery stable, his pistol already gripped in his hand. A fourth watching from the window of the barber shop, head and shoulders showing over the curtain that was draped across, weapon hidden.

The blast of the shotgun tore the morning apart.

One of the men who'd ridden in with Herne was hurled forward on to the neck of his horse, legs kicking up behind him and arms flung out. The back of his shirt was little more than thin shreds of blue that were already disappearing into a morass of flayed flesh and streaming blood. The animal bucked and twisted beneath him and threw him, face down, to the dusty street.

The second man had been facing, unknowingly, the direction from which the shotgun blast was to come. A rash of shot whipped through his face, making him instantly beyond recognition. In places he was cleaned to the bone. Pieces of tissue as large as silver dollars were hurled through the air. Grey matter from his brain skidded over the uneven boards of the sidewalk and stopped against the preacher's right shoe.

The girl screamed and threw herself inside the protection of her mother's arms.

'Jesus damn it!'

Charlie Bowdre flung himself from his saddle, hitting the dirt hard and rolling painfully over to his right, his fingers fumbling for his gun. A pistol shot skipped earth up into his face and momentarily blinded him.

Herne swung his mount about, guiding it with knees and boots, hand clawing for his Colt and arcing it clear and up. He saw the ends of the shotgun's barrels being pulled hastily out of sight and sent a quick shot tearing through the inch of wood at the bottom of the window frame.

A woman's voice was screaming, high-pitched and loud, and it was impossible to tell if it were the mother or the daughter.

Another rifle shot came from the corner of alley and street and this one splintered away an end-strut from the back of the preacher's wagon. Boots slapped the street dirt hard and fast and the man from the opposite end of town headed towards the still sprawling figure of Charlie Bowdre.

Herne saw him coming, called a warning to Charlie, and went back to his own affairs. He shot through the open window as the shotgun began to push back out and was disappointed not to hear a man shout in pain. But the weapon was withdrawn.

Charlie wriggled through forty-five degrees and rested his right arm on the elbow and fired twice. The first slug whined away harmlessly, the second shattered the running man's left shinbone and drove him through a half-circle. The leg kicked up behind him and the man collapsed, lopsidedly. Charlie set the fingers of his left hand about his right wrist to steady his aim and sent a bullet into the man's side. The body jerked a couple of feet as if a mule had kicked into it and then seemed to be still.

On the sidewalk the preacher had pulled his womenfolk into the store for safety and now stood in the doorway, his bible thrust outwards towards the street.

Herne ran to the side of the flat-bed wagon and ducked down against one of the wheels. Seconds later a pistol bullet drove into one of the spokes and ricochetted away, sending splinters against Herne's back and his left shoulder. He fired once at the alley corner, once at the upstairs window and jumped up on to the wagon, rolling fast across it and knocking parcels and packages asunder. He came down on the other side, landing on his knees, right arm resting on the edge of the wagon and his head ducked down behind it, taking aim.

The shot gun appeared at the window and Herne hesitated, waited, saw a few inches of the man's head, neck, shoulders: Herne fired.

The double barrels angled steeply up into the air and the head was blasted back and away. This time there was a scream of agony but Herne was moving too fast to hear it.

Charlie's shout had spun him about and flat on to the dirt of the street. Charlie fired over Herne's head, once only, enough to send the man with the rifle sliding back from sight.

'Jed?'

'Yeah?'

'He the only one?'

Herne got to one knee and glanced up at the window. No one else had taken the bushwacker's place.

'Guess so.'

'Let's get the bastard.'

Herne slid fresh cartridges down into the chambers of the Colt and looked over his shoulder. His gaze was held by the spectacle of the preacher in the store doorway, his wife and daughter looking, despite themselves, through the glass.

'Okay, Charlie.'

Herne stood up and moved to the wall. Up and down the street anxious and interested faces peered from what cover they could find. The bodies of the three dead men lay like bloodied islands adrift in the wide stretch of packed dirt and mud.

In the hushed air of anticipation that followed his slow progress towards the head of the alley, Herne heard the clear sounds of a horse and rider moving away fast.

He stopped and turned his head. 'Hear that?'

'Yeah. Best be sure though.'

'Uh-huh.'

Herne was level with the barber's shop when some instinct made him swing his head. He saw the shape of the man – only a spectator like so many others – yet there was something about the stance that warned him. That moment the glass at the front of the barber shop exploded outwards and Herne crouched against the planking of the wall and fired. Once – the fragments of glass still flying through the air like a flock of startled, translucent birds – twice – the glass settling, the man pitching forward through the shop front and staggering over the boardwalk.

Both Herne and Charlie waited, weapons at the ready.

The man pitched on to the hitching rail between two horses which shifted uneasily away and allowed him to fold his body round the rail. For several seconds he swung there, hung there, then somersaulted over and landed with his arms almost straight back past his head, one leg stretched wide to the side and the other buckled beneath him.

'Check the alley, Charlie,' said Herne and walked to where the man lay.

He recognized him as being one of the Dolan followers who'd been involved in the shoot-out at McSween's. He didn't think he knew any of the others.

'Clear, Jed. He's skipped out.'

Herne holstered his Colt while Charlie went to retrieve

their horses. The black-hatted preacher had come to the edge of the boardwalk and stood with his bible pressed against his black heart, right hand outstretched towards the dead and words of prayer loud from his lips.

The girl, face whiter now inside its frame of black hair, stood in the shop doorway and stared down at the splatterings of red and grey that spread over the boards.

Chapter Five

Herne didn't think a lot more about the girl the rest of that summer. There were too many other things demanding his attention. The attempted ambush in Lincoln sparked off a series of irregular outbursts between the two factions which resulted in a good many wounded and not a few dead. Those who'd reckoned the Lincoln County War to be over seemed to have been misinformed.

But gradually, as the fierceness of the New Mexico summer began to temper down, things eased off. Incidents were no more than isolated sparks. The big ranchers and the beef contractors were coming to terms: there was too much money to be made, too much profit being lost, too many government contracts that had to be filled.

Herne and Charlie Bowdre rode out one morning early in the fall and headed down towards the Hondo river. They part had in mind doing a little hunting, but more than anything staying cooped up with the Kid was getting to them so's they needed to feel a lot of space around them. Space and air. They let their mounts have their heads, galloping freely across the scrub between sage and saltbush, the rhythm of the animals' bodies driving up through their own, the wind racing.

Finally the two men slowed and steered the horses along the rise of a slope of land topped with half a dozen black oaks, their evergreen leaves spreading wide from smooth pale bark.

'Hell, Jed, that was somethin'.'

Herne leaned over the neck of his mount and tried to control his breathing. 'Sure . . . was. Better'n . . .'

'Yeah.'

Bowdre swung down from the saddle. 'Take a spell?'

'Sure.'

Herne dismounted and both men loosened the girths under their saddles. Bowdre took down his water canteen and had a quick swallow before passing it over. Herne removed his hat and let it fall to the floor before accepting a drink. Sweat stuck both men's clothes fast to their bodies.

'You hangin' on long?' asked Bowdre, sitting down at the foot of one of the oaks and leaning his back against it.

Herne looked at him. He'd wondered how much Charlie wanted to talk about leaving. It was common gossip that he had a Mexican wife called Manuela. When a bunch of them, including Billy, Bowdre and Herne, had lit out for the border after an earlier incident in the war, Charlie Bowdre had left them heading south and ridden to visit Manuela.

Herne didn't understand what kept him from being with her all the time. He'd even thought about asking, but had shied clear. Charlie was a pretty even-tempered man, but ragging him about his Mexican wife was a sure way to get him fighting mad.

Not that Jed Herne thought too much about having a wife anyway, just that if you had one it made more sense to live together rather than apart.

Herne waited for Bowdre to continue.

'I was thinkin' . . . don't seem a whole lot of point in hangin' around. We ain't goin' to be welcome on the payroll once they're certain it's cowhands they need an' not such as you 'n' me.'

Herne squatted on the ground, taking off his bandanna and wiping the sweat away from his neck 'You're thinkin' right. Seems to me. We better go afore we're pushed.'

'Yeah.' Charlie gave a short laugh and dug down into the soil with the heel of his boot. 'Sometimes I reckon I should've lit out a long time back. Like that feller who faced off Billy the time Billy was drunk.'

'Hart, you mean?'

'That's him. Wes Hart. Just up and rode out an' kept

goin'. Billy didn't like that. Sent me an' Dan Halloran after him. Followed him right up into Indian Territory. He was workin' as a deputy, had been when we caught up with him.'

Herne nodded. He remembered Wes Hart: a tall, mean bastard with faded blue eyes, a mother-of-pearl grip on his Colt Peacemaker and a sawn-off 10-gauge shotgun.

'Halloran never come back from that, did he?' Herne said.

Bowdre shook his head. 'I was all for talkin' Hart into ridin' back with us an' if he stood fast leavin' it at that. Dan, he took it more serious. Made a play for his gun.' Bowdre paused and looked at Herne. 'Hart killed him.'

'Yeah,' said Herne softly. He was certain he would have done the same.

'He helped me throw Dan over his horse and I rode off and buried him out by this creek. Came back.'

'Maybe you should've stayed.'

'Maybe.'

Both men were silent for a while, the only sound that of the horses pulling down at the leaves of the oak.

'Reckon I'll give it another couple of days,' said Herne finally. 'Then drift west, see if I can pick up work.'

'Arizona?'

'Good as any.'

'Yeah.' Bowdre hacked out more earth.

'How 'bout you?'

Charlie Bowdre glanced across and shrugged his shoulders and said, 'You know how it is with me. Me an' Manuela.'

He turned his head away and scratched at his left shoulder. It was the first time Herne had ever heard him mention his wife's name of his own choice.

'Charlie . . .' he began.

'Yeah?'

'Oh, hell, nothin'.' Herne straightened and stretched the muscles in his legs. 'What say we move on?'

'Okay.'

They cut down across their earlier trail, making for the river. Before long they could see it blue against the reddish-yellow mud of its flat banks, a slow and shallow path of water travelling down from the Sacramento mountains to the west towards the River Pecos.

Some little way along the buildings of the town of Hondo showed dark in the yellow light.

There was a gathering down by the river.

Voices lifted to them.

We'll all gather at the river
The beautiful, the beautiful river
We'll all gather at the river
That flows by the throne of God

There were around twenty folk down at the water's edge, mostly women and children, a scattering of men, and with them a few dogs and horses and a couple of mules. Herne recognized the flat-bed wagon before he picked out the preacher.

Without even wanting to, his eyes searched the small crowd for the girl, but she didn't appear to be there. Neither did her mother. The preacher raised both hands for silence as the hymn came to an end. He took off his black coat and handed it to a woman standing close and then turned and waded out into the Hondo. He went on into the water until it lapped around his thighs. Then he held the bible aloft and began to address the congregation.

'Ain't that . . . ?' Bowdre began.

'Yeah.'

'We ain't goin' down there, are we?'

'Passin' by.'

Bowdre gave Herne a hasty glance to make sure he wasn't joking, but he saw that Herne was serious. So he shrugged his shoulders, touched his spurs to his mount and followed Herne down.

One of the women had waded out after the preacher

and now she was standing before him, her skirts soaked through, the water well to her waist. The preacher held the bible out at an angle with his left hand and set the palm of the right against the woman's head.

Her eyes were closed and there was a look of anticipation on her face that betokened fear or excitement of another kind.

Suddenly there was a mighty splashing and a roar went up from those watching and the preacher had ducked the woman into the water, head first, and seemed to be holding her under. The crowd cheered and cries of 'Amen' mingled with those of 'Hallelujah'.

'Jed, he's done drownin' her!' shouted Charlie Bowdre.

Herne shook his head. 'No, he ain't. He's savin' her.'

Bowdre scratched his shoulder and shook his head from side to side and said: 'If that ain't the darndest way of savin' a woman I ever saw. How the hell's she goin' to breathe under that muddy water?'

The woman burst back through the surface and rolls of ripples spread away towards both shores.

The preacher turned his face to heaven and lifted both hands towards it also, their palms outspread, the bible resting on the open left hand.

The woman stood in front of him, eyes still closed, hair matted to her head and water dripping from her face.

Then both of the preacher's hands returned to her head and the bible was pressed against her and the crowd sang out praises, and hymns were started and faded and fresh ones took their place. 'Amen, Amen, Amen.'

The baptized woman opened her eyes and saw the preacher standing with her in the river and listened to the words he spoke through the joyous clamour from the shore. After several moments she began to sway and her head lolled to one side and she fell forwards into the preacher's arms. He bent below the surface of the water and scooped her up into his arms and began to wade with her towards the shore.

'Let's go, Charlie,' said Herne, flicking out the reins.

'Where to, Jed? We headin' back?'

'Not yet. We'll take a little ride into Hondo.'

Charlie Bowdre looked at the back of Herne's head, shrugged, scratched and followed.

The main street in Hondo was twice as wide as the river after which the town was named. Squat adobes lined it haphazardly, square and low. Here and there a wooden building had been erected with lumber that had mostly been freighted down from the north or east. It was a lazy fall day in town and the only excitement was the baptism going on outside the town limits. About all that stirred in the main street was a dog the colour of light chocolate which ran around chasing its tail and never quite catching it.

When Herne and Bowdre appeared, the dog forgot its tail for a time and sat back and barked at them, running quickly towards the horses and then backing off again at a curse from Charlie and a flash of his boot.

'Sure looks lively, don't it?' grinned Charlie.

'Uh-huh.'

'Reckon they got a saloon here?'

Herne gestured down the street. 'Sign there.'

When they reached it, it read, 'Harding's Store – dry goods, clothing, boots, saddles, guns and ammunition'. The words were spelt right but they sloped down the sign as if they'd been set there by a man who was in the action of very slowly falling over.

'Every damn thing but liquor,' said Bowdre and looked around for something more promising.

'Help you, gents?'

Neither Herne nor Bowdre had spotted the man opening the door to the store and they faced round sharp when they heard the high, slightly whining voice.

Harding was maybe an inch above five foot and that had made him the tallest of his family by more than a foot.

His folk had been circus performers in Europe, working as clowns and tumblers and jugglers and none of them any more than dwarfs. One night, it was suspected, Harding's mother had strayed behind the big top with Zoltan the Magnificent who bent iron bars between his teeth and lifted gigantic weights on the back of his neck. The result of this unlikely coupling had been Harding – though, of course, that hadn't been his name. He'd read it on the side of a wagon when he was starting out on the Oregon trail. Harding had never made it to Oregon. Fate had instead sent him south and west and he'd thought of California and landed up in New Mexico with some money still in his right shoe and a flair for five card stud. In his first week in Santa Fe Harding had won so much at poker it had been wise to leave town. Hondo had seemed far enough from anywhere to be safe. He'd invested his money in a store and now when there weren't any customers, which was quite often, he did his best to lure occasional travellers in off the street to play cards with him. All the other residents had already learned the little man's prowess the hard way and none of them would play with him any more.

'Passing through?'

They looked down at him and said nothing.

'If you're taking a breather, maybe you'd care to step inside. Might be a few supplies you need, fill your canteens free . . . hand of stud to pass a little time?'

He gazed up at them hopefully, his nose twitching slightly like a gun dog that senses the closeness of its quarry.

'We was wantin' a drink,' said Charlie. 'Beer.'

'Well . . .' began Harding doubtfully.

'You sell beer?'

'No, not exactly.'

'Well, then,' said Charlie, 'where exactly does?'

Harding bit his upper lip and frowned. 'Place down the street, they got beer but it don't taste much.'

'More taste 'n water?' said Charlie Bowdre.

Harding shook his head and looked resigned to missing

out on a possible hand of stud. 'Don't bank on it,' he said. 'Don't bank on it.'

In the event he was three-parts right. What the saloon served for beer was so watered down that little of the original taste remained: what did, assured Herne and Bowdre they were still getting the best of the deal. The beer seemed to have been made from old corn husks mashed in with lye soap and then swilled around in a horse trough for a while.

Herne kept going until his third mouthful, then spat it out over the sawdust-spotted floor.

'Hogwash!' he called out to the mostly empty room.

The barkeep swatted a fly away from his head and leaned himself awake. 'You want some more?' he asked vaguely.

Charlie held his glass high and tipped it so that what remained poured on to the floor and ran between a gap in the boards.

'Hey!' called the bartender. 'That's good beer you're wastin'.'

'Uh-uh,' said Herne, standing up. 'You ain't but nearly right. It's beer, maybe, but good beer it definitely ain't.'

A black and white cat missing most of its left ear and with a variety of scabs about the rest of its face, wandered over from a corner and started to lap up the beer before it ran away.

'Watch out for that animal now,' said Charlie by the door. 'It's gonna fall down an' die inside around five minutes from now.'

The barkeep shuffled along the bar a ways and coughed. 'You ain't tryin' to be funny, now, mister, are you?'

Neither Charlie Bowdre nor Herne thought it was worth trying to explain: beside they weren't really being funny at all.

'You think that feller back at the store's any good?' asked Charlie as they stood by their horses, prepared to remount.

'At stud?'

'Yeah.'

Herne set his head to one side and grinned. 'I'd say he's either poor as that beer we just paid for an' threw away, else he's sharper'n a barber's fresh-stropped razor.'

Charlie Bowdre's eyes lit up. 'You want to find out?'

Herne was about to shake his head when he thought, why not? There wasn't a hurry to get back to where they'd come from and since they'd ridden as far as Hondo they might as well sample a little more of what it offered.

'Why not?' he said.

Bowdre laughed and slapped his leg and they led their horses back across the street.

The diminutive storekeeper was as pleased to see them as if they'd been carrying sacks of gold dust and a sign that said 'Help Yourself'. He insisted on giving them sourdough biscuits to eat, setting a fresh pot of coffee on his stove and wiping the seats of the chairs before Herne and Bowdre sat down. He fetched a new deck of cards from the shelves and smiled and chattered and smiled and cut and shuffled the deck as fast as Herne himself could clear leather.

Herne glanced at Charlie, who was still managing to look hopeful, but himself he realized already that they were on to a lost cause. Just half an hour later, so did Charlie. Harding had stripped him of most all his wages and was set to take everything from his saddle to his boots if Charlie didn't watch out. Herne played more carefully, throwing in early and only gambling on the few certainties that either luck or Harding's dealing had allowed him.

'Maybe, Charlie, we ought to know when we're licked,' said Herne, while the storekeeper was taking a break and reaching the pot from the stove.

'Hell, Jed, I want to earn back what I've lost.'

Herne laughed. 'No way you're doin' that if we sit here till sun-up day after tomorrow. He's slicker'n a tomcat in a storm.'

'But, Jed . . .'

Harding handed them mugs of coffee and smiled

ingratiatingly. 'Gents, you are surely not thinking of leaving. Not when the game has only just started.'

''Fraid so,' said Herne quickly. 'See, my friend an' I, we ain't in your league. You already took Charlie here for most every dime he's got. I don't imagine you want to play for matches, now, do you?'

Harding did not. He was very unhappy about the turn of events but the way the two strangers wore their guns advised him it was better not to protest too forcefully. If only, though, he'd had as much time again, he could have cleaned them both out.

Herne swallowed some of the coffee, made a face on account of it being both too hot and too bitter, and nodded at Bowdre. 'Let's go.'

He turned from the small table and as he did so the door opened and the girl came in. Something hit Herne high in the left side, like a fist. Her face was pale and pretty and the width of her mouth already promised something that perhaps the rest of her body only knew in dreams. She recognized him, too, and almost let slip the parcel she was holding in her hand.

With a small gasp she clasped it against herself.

'Miss Louise,' said the storekeeper.

Louise, thought Herne, that's her name.

'Jed, we . . .' Charlie started, but Herne hardly heard him.

'I came to . . . my mother asked me . . .' Her cheeks glowed under Herne's stare. 'Could you see that this gets on the stage tomorrow? It's some tracts of my father's. He . . .'

Abruptly she set the brown-paper bundle on the counter and went out. Herne drew his breath and went after her. She was a half-dozen yards into the street, hurrying away, head down.

'Miss.'

Her step faltered but slowly her head turned, dark hair bobbing.

'A month or more back – in Lincoln – you was there with your folks and . . .'

'And you killed two men.'

'Yes, I . . . it wasn't none of my doin'. You must've seen that.'

'Your gun went off by itself?'

'I didn't mean that.' Herne hadn't expected it to be like this, hadn't anticipated that she would be so firm, aggressive. He had imagined her shy, gentle, like a young rabbit with startled eyes and fear in its heart.

'What did you want to say to me?' She was blushing and her hands were nervous at her sides, but her voice was clear and loud enough and she would not look away from him now. Look evil in the eye, her father had taught her and she knew her father regarded men like this one as evil.

'That I . . . do you live here? In Hondo? You and your folks?'

'Yes.'

Herne hesitated. He knew that Charlie had come out of the store behind him and was standing listening.

'My mother will be expecting me back home,' the girl said, turning to go.

Herne glanced awkwardly round and saw the ear-to-ear grin spread round Charlie's face. He hurried closer to the girl, further from Charlie's hearing.

'That time in Lincoln,' he said hastily, 'when I saw you I thought . . .' He broke off as if realizing the futility of what he was doing. He saw himself in her eyes, an aging gunfighter with lank, greasy hair and saddle-stained clothes: a man more than twice her age.

Herne turned away. 'It don't matter.'

He heard a soft movement behind him and turned towards it.

Her eyes were bright and dark.

'I thought you was prettier than any other girl I'd ever seen.'

She stilled her hand on its way to her face.

'An' not only that, somethin' different too. I don't know, somethin' I never saw in a girl before.'

She smiled the briefest of smiles and there was a sign of sadness at the corners of her wide mouth. 'I shall have to go.'

'An' if I come and see you again.'

'Again?'

'I'm here now.'

She fidgeted with the ends of her hair.

'My father would never allow it. He was in Lincoln when you killed those men.' She paused. 'He knows who you are.'

'Then you . . .'

'I must go.' She lifted her skirt with one hand and, turning away, began to run, lightly, down the wide street. Small puffs of dust sprang up behind her. Herne watched until she was out of sight.

Charlie Bowdre was already mounted and he passed the reins of Herne's horse down to him. The storekeeper stood against the frame of his doorway, chewing on a length of liquorice root. The light chocolate coloured dog lay on its back, rolling this way and that, scratching out fleas.

Herne said nothing, mounted up and began to ride away.

It was a good three miles before Charlie Bowdre dared to speak. When he did it was with a broad grin and a wave of his hand and: 'Just ain't your day, Jed. Hell, you wasn't lucky in cards either!'

Herne didn't think that was at all funny.

Chapter Six

'You heard the Kid's headin' out t'Fort Sumner?'

'Yeah.'

'Place draws him like a fly.'

'Seems.'

Charlie Bowdre passed the bottle, but Herne shook his head and Charlie shrugged and had another swallow: it did taste pretty bad at that.

'You ain't thinkin' of taggin' along?'

'Uh-uh.'

Charlie cleared his throat and spat down into the ground, the ball rolling and gathering dust until it stopped, choked.

'You mind sayin' just what you are intendin' doin'?'

Herne eased up the stained brim of his stetson and peered up at Bowdre. 'Little of this, little of that.'

Bowdre laughed. 'Now what in the Lord's name does that mean?'

'I mean, what are you goin' to do? You can't stay here. Less you're lookin' to punch cattle. That don't seem in your line of work too easy.'

Herne stood up and walked away from the corral fence. 'Charlie, why don't you saddle up and ride down to that wife of yours and stop persecutin' me with your fool questions?'

'On account of I don't like to see no friend of mine make a fool of hisself.'

'Now what does that mean?'

'It means, 's if you didn't know, I reckon you're lookin' to go sneakin' round Hondo like a rooster on the prowl an' all you're goin' to get for it is a flea in your ear. That's what.'

Herne made a pattern in the dirt with the toe of his scuffed boot. Rubbed the palm of his right hand against the edge of his Colt butt. Said nothing.

'See. I'm right, ain't I? Ain't I?'

Herne came at him so fast that Bowdre all but dropped his whisky bottle.

'Charlie, you either drunk too much of that rotgut or you didn't drink enough yet. I never heard you go blabbin' on at the mouth like this all the time we been ridin' together. Now quit an' get packed out of here and go see Manuela.'

Charlie Bowdre opened his mouth to say something in reply, but the look in Herne's eyes told him he'd be best advised to say nothing. The mouth drew in a little air and closed again, silent.

A while later, Bowdre was sitting astride his horse, saddle bags bulging and his bedroll tied on top of them.

'Jed.'

Herne reached up and shook the man's hand.

'Charlie.'

'Ride easy.'

Herne released Charlie's hand. 'Sure. You take care. See to that wife of yours.'

Charlie turned the horse away and looked over his shoulder. 'You give my regards to that little girl of yours – if you can get close enough.'

Charlie Bowdre laughed and slapped his hand down on the animal's rump and rode away. Herne sat up on the fence and watched him go, never looking back. He never saw him again. Three years later he heard that for whatever reason Bowdre had made his way back north to Fort Sumner and ran with a gang of cattle rustlers. They got themselves trapped by Pat Garrett and a posse at Stinking Springs round the Christmas of 1880. Charlie took seven slugs before he died. They buried him at Fort Sumner close by Billy Bonney.

One way or another Pat Garrett had a lot to answer for.

The same day Bowdre rode south to his wife, Herne stashed his few possessions on his horse, drew the last of his pay, and rode north. He wasn't about to admit to himself that he was hanging around just so's to be near enough to the girl to get another chance to see her, but he certainly wasn't heading far off.

He soon swung out east, keeping the tops of the Capitan mountains well to his left. There was enough money in his pockets to keep him free and independent for a matter of weeks, but that wasn't going to be enough. Not for what Herne had in mind. He reined in the horse and ran place names through his mind. He'd been talking with Chisum one time and Chisum had said . . . yes, Mesa. Forty or so miles to the north-east between Lincoln and Fort Sumner. A town where a man with a lot of sand could earn himself good bounty. Almost as many desperadoes hanging out in there as there were in Fort Sumner.

'Or down here working for you,' Herne had commented, and Chisum had given that a good belly laugh and clapped Herne on the shoulder.

Mesa.

Well, that was where Herne needed to go.

The sunbaked scrubland offered nothing in the way of shelter. Herne let his animal have its head, choosing its own pace, stopping now and then to give them both a few moments respite before continuing. The sun beat down as hot as if it was still full summer and not coming into fall.

Not that there was much out in that flatland to fall.

Saltbush and creosote and sage.

Gophers and rabbits and snakes.

Herne thought about Louise as he rode, recalling the way her dark curls framed her face, the spunky way she'd talked back at him – the way he'd felt seeing her again, sudden.

Mesa shimmered out of the desert like some mirage: only it was real. A tumbledown place that seemed to have been set out there in the middle of nothing and nowhere just to be perverse. The only reason Herne could figure out for a man going there was either that he was lost or that he wanted to be some place other men wouldn't easily find him.

Like Hondo, it was a mixture of adobes and wooded shacks, but these were in worse repair, crumbling and falling apart even though some of them had likely not been put up more than a year or two at most. The main street was wide as most, but short, with a well at the far end and buildings around it forming three parts of a circle.

Behind and between the buildings there were tents, patched and re-patched, buckets and barrels haphazardly around them.

Men sat on the remains of what had once been a boardwalk along the right-hand side of the street and watched Herne ride in.

They were used to riders who looked much as Herne did, drifters and no-accounts whose clothes were trail-stained and whose mounts were smeared with dust and sweat and who toted guns like they knew how to use them and would at the least opportunity. Men who rode with little account of the law, even though there were times when they claimed to be about its business.

Men like Pat Garrett.

Men like Herne the Hunter

Unlike Hondo, Mesa wasn't parched for saloons. Herne rode past the Three Deuces, past the Yellow Dog and drew to a halt outside the Swados House. He dismounted and tied his reins to the hitching rail and pushed the single door aside.

The bar was a trestle table set at the far end of the room between stacks of boxes. A few tables were scattered around the room, along with some large barrels which were performing the same function. Half a dozen men were sitting over their glasses and they all stopped whatever they were doing when Herne came in and turned towards him. In Mesa you didn't look away from strangers – not at first – not until they'd proved that was the best thing to do.

Herne stood just inside the door a few moments, returning the stares, checking out that there was no one present that he knew.

One man, a thin half-breed Mex with a pencil-thin moustache and a soiled embroidered waistcoat, held his attention longer than the rest.

Dodge.

Wichita.

Ellsworth.

It seemed strange to place a Mex so far north but in the back of his mind Herne could see the man's face, the same insolent stare, in another saloon, larger and more crowded.

The man knew him, too, he was certain of that.

As for the others, they meant nothing to him. Keeping one eye on the Mex, Herne walked down the room to the bar. A fat man with very little hair on his head and a surprisingly small mouth, nodded towards Herne and reached for a glass.

'Just rode in?' The voice was thin and weak as the mouth, as if it wasn't the fat man talking at all, but some midget trapped inside him.

'Beer,' said Herne and tossed a coin down on to the trestle table.

'Hot, ain't it?' said the fat man with the thin voice.

Herne took the beer, brushed a hand across the top to remove the wash of froth and drank half of it down in a swallow.

'Guess you must've ridden quite a ways.'

Herne drank the remainder of the beer in another swallow and set the glass back on the table.

'Another?' asked the fat man.

Herne turned round and walked back out into the street.

He still couldn't remember exactly where he'd seen the Mex.

He untied his horse and led it down the street towards the well. A group of men were sitting on the crumbling adobe wall around it and swapping yarns about the fights they'd been in and the women they'd never lain with but liked to brag that they had.

When Herne came towards them they stopped telling stories and looked him over. One of them recognized him right off. He'd been in a one-horse town on the Arizona border, oh, it could be five years back and, of course, he'd looked a mite younger then, but still there was no mistaking the way he walked, his face, that lank dark hair to his shoulders.

'Herne the Hunter.'

'Herne the Hunter.'

The name ran from mouth to mouth, from man to man. To one or two, it didn't mean a thing, others knew it vaguely from rumour and nothing more. To most, though, it meant they were watching one of the most feared guns on the frontier: railroad trouble-shooter, bounty hunter, hired gun. A man whose reputation with the Colt he wore strapped to his side was second to none and level with the best.

Herne the Hunter.

He stopped short of the well and retethered his mount outside the adobe with the sign attached to the wall reading: Town Marshal.

Seth Sheperd had been working both sides of the law for all forty years of his life – or so it seemed whenever he stuck his feet up on the scarred desk in his office and thought back. He'd stole his first gold when he was but six years old, stabbed his first man – who was a woman – when he was nine. Come his thirteenth birthday he was running with the Morrel gang down by Nogales and on his fourteenth birthday they hit his first-ever bank. All that was a long time ago and now Sheperd was too tired to do anything much other than try to stay alive.

When he'd taken the marshal's job in Mesa he'd known it was akin to taking the marshal's job in Hell.

Hell! There hadn't been a lot else to choose.

He reached for the Colt Peacemaker he kept on the desk

top as soon as he heard the steps approach. By the time Herne had opened the door and stepped inside the hammer of the marshal's pistol was thumbed back and the barrel was pointing to a spot not unadjacent to Herne's heart.

'Marshal.'

'You want to shut that door.'

Herne kicked it shut without turning round.

'Now just as long as you're here, lift that gun out of your holster and set it down on my desk. Easy like.'

Herne hesitated under the stare of the marshal's gun.

'Only rule I got in town,' said Sheperd. 'Like to make sure when I talk to a man he ain't gonna draw on me and get things messed up in here.' He chuckled and the chuckle became a raw cough but the gun hand didn't shake more than a fraction.

Herne used finger and thumb to lift the Colt .45 clear and he set it down where the marshal indicated.

'There. That makes me feel a whole lot better.' Sheperd released the hammer on his own gun and lowered it, but kept his fingers about the butt. 'Now what can I do for Jed Herne?'

Herne raised his eyebrows enquiringly.

'Don't act surprised. You got yourself quite a reputation. It's a wonder some punk ain't called you out down some alley and put a slug in your back afore you got the chance to turn round. Just to make a name for hisself.'

'Yeah,' agreed Herne. 'A couple tried.'

The marshal chuckled.

'I heard you was down with the Kid,' he said after a couple of moments.

'Was.'

'Uh-huh. Hell of a business, way I heard it.'

'Yeah.'

'You just left Lincoln?'

Herne nodded. 'Yeah.'

'Then you didn't ride here by chance. You sure didn't come for the scenery.'

'No.'

Seth Sheperd set the Colt Peacemaker down on the desk, close by Herne's pistol. He unbuttoned the top two buttons of his vest and pushed a hand up through his greying hair. The eyes that looked at Herne were grey, watery at the corners. The skin around them was wrinkled like snake skin.

'Lookin' for someone?'

Herne nodded. 'Could be.'

'What's that mean?'

'Means it depends who you got.'

Sheperd whistled softly and pointed to the chair over by the side wall. 'Best take the weight off'n your legs a while. We'll talk about this.'

Herne didn't see a lot of point in discussing the matter, but he didn't want to get on the marshal's wrong side – not as long as it might be avoided. He pulled the chair over closer to the desk and sat down.

The marshal eased back one of the desk drawers and felt around under some papers for the bottle. He passed it to Herne first, holding the stopper back in his left hand.

'Good whisky,' the marshal promised.

Herne sampled it and he wasn't lying. He had a little taste more and passed it back. Sheperd poured himself a generous shot into a chipped mug and leaned back on the hind legs of his chair, cup in hand.

'You're looking for bounty.' It didn't come out like a question.

'Yeah, that's right.'

'How come?'

'How come any man goes after bounty? I want the money. Need it.'

Sheperd drank some of his whisky, washing it around inside his mouth before swallowing. 'Must be easier ways.'

'None quicker.'

'Uum.' He took another drink and let the chair settle

back down. 'I want to explain something to you. This town's got more wanted men and roughnecks in it than most, but it's also got a marshal. That ain't normal but the reason's straightforward enough. Every flier I get I stuff down in one of these here drawers an' I don't take it back out. Any man who comes to Mesa knows that an' he also knows there's a little debt he's got to pay. He keeps whatever robbin' and such he's doing out of town.

' 'Course, with so many hotheads around, there's fights enough, but usually they keep it amongst themselves. I been here getting on two years and I've got things runnin' pretty much the way I wants 'em.'

He broke off for another drink and stared over at Herne's impassive face.

'I don't want you ridin' in here and throwin' the whole works out the window. You understand that?'

Herne said, 'What happens when a United States marshal comes through?'

'Hell, that's different. I got no way of standin' out against him and everyone else understands that. US marshal rides this way they clear out or take their chances.'

'Then they can take their chances with me just the same.'

'Ain't the same.' Sheperd shook his head.

Herne stood back up. 'Too bad.'

'I could stop you.'

'You could shit!'

Sheperd started to go for his gun but thought better of it almost as soon as his hand began to move. He knew that if Herne was even three parts as good as his reputation, he wouldn't stand a chance. A man like Herne only agreed to give over his gun as long as he knew he could take it back with no problem.

'Best let me see them fliers,' Herne said.

Sheperd sucked in his cheeks and finished his drink. He put the cup down by the two pistols and pulled open a drawer. He took a haphazard bundle of hand bills out and dropped them across the desk.

'Sort 'em through,' he said, and moved away to give Herne room.

Some of the bills had a sketch of the wanted man or woman underneath the word 'Wanted', most just had the name and a description and an account of what crime had been carried out. The most important part for Herne was the sum of money capture would provide.

Herne leafed through the names. There were Casey Dilkes and Nevada Raikes, wanted for robbery and rustling; Shorty Long, who held up a bank in Sedalia and got away with two thousand dollars; Deedee Palmer, who shot a man playing cards and took off with the pot; Dutch Daley the Butcher, who put his trade to good use when he raped a couple of women on the New Mexico-Arizona border and then dismembered the bodies; the One-Eyed Kid, wanted for murder and bank robbery; Spanish Joe LeFarge, who held up the Aitcheson, Topeka and Santa Fe railroad twice on the same stretch of track within a fortnight; Slanting Annie, who was wanted for burglary; Baldy McDowell, who raided an Apache reservation, shot and killed or wounded some dozen braves, murdered the agency chief and stole all the supplies of beef and blankets; Shorty Russell and China Mike, wanted for rustling cattle; Sissy Foustone, who held up the Santa Fe stage and shot the driver through the foot before riding off with the strong box; the McCandles family, who were wanted on seven separate counts of armed robbery; Highhat Dixon, Jerry Molar, the Arapahoe Kid, the Carter brothers, Wild Bill Nelson, Two-fingered Jack Slattery, Pierce Latham.

Herne shuffled the fliers back into some sort of order and pulled one off the top.

'He around?'

'Latham?'

'Uh-huh.'

Sheperd pushed at a gap between his teeth with the end of his tongue, trying to force out a fragment of beef that had been stuck there since the previous night. He poured himself another drink into the chipped cup and offered the bottle to Herne.

Herne declined. 'Don't waste my time, Marshal.'

Sheperd had some of the whisky. 'He's here. But what in God's name you want to mess with him for?'

Herne held up the hand bill. 'Thousand dollars.'

The sketch of Pierce Latham showed a lean face with deep-sunk eyes and thick stubble, a mean mouth and a lock of dark hair that fell down almost dead centre on his forehead. He was wanted for killing a United States deputy marshal on Easter Day of eighteen seventy eight out at the Basque Redondo. His other offences included stagecoach robbery, bank robbery and two other murders. All of these offences were committed along with the rest of the Latham gang, most of whom had since been captured.

'He's a mean-looking bastard, sure enough,' said Sheperd.

'He don't look as mean as he is.'

'Know him?'

'Saw him pistol whip a woman most to death one time.'

Sheperd whistled shrilly. 'Thought you said something about this being an easy way to get money.'

'It's fast. Federal offence, you can draw money for the reward from the bank, can't you?'

'Yeah.'

'Well, then, that's an end to it.'

Herne rolled up the poster and stuck it in his back pants pocket.

Sheperd combed through his hair with the fingers of his left hand at the same time as bringing the chipped cup to his mouth with the other. A whoop of laughter rose up from the street and faded.

'Okay if I take my gun? Guess we've finished here.'

'Sure. Only . . .'

'What?'

'Latham ain't goin' to be easy.'

Herne lifted the Colt from the table and weighed it in

his hand for a moment, enjoying the perfect balance. 'I know that. Else someone'd've ridden in before now. Thousand dollars is a lot of money.'

'You know he's got kin?'

Herne nodded. 'Heard they were locked away in the state penitentiary.'

'That's right. Ezekiel, Damon and Howie, they're his brothers. Billy Dean Latham, he's some kind of cousin. They're all inside. There's another cousin called Mason or some such, he's on the run an' I don't know where.'

'Know where I'll find Pierce?'

'Not for sure. Was sleeping with a woman over the Three Deuces, but I heard he moved on. He'll be around, though. Likes to drink come sundown. Deuces or the Swados House. You look for him, you'll find him.'

Herne moved towards the door and touched his fingers to the underside of his hat brim.

'Marshal?'

'Yeah?'

'I saw a breed Mex when I rode in, moustache and one of them short jackets. Know him?'

Sheperd considered it for a few moments, then sat back down behind his desk. 'Sounds like Sanchez.'

'Who's he run with?'

'No one special. Came in with a bunch of drifters who rode up over the border maybe a month back, but he's been around a long time. Just drifting. Nothing special.' He looked at Herne questioningly. 'How come the interest?'

Herne shrugged. 'Seen him somewhere Kansas way an' I can't remember where.'

'Yeah, that's one of the troubles with living too long. Things get kind of blurred.' He grinned and pointed at the bottle. 'One for the trail?'

Herne shook his head. 'I'll take one when I bring Latham in.'

'Dead or alive?'

'Dead or alive.'

Herne opened the door.

'One thing I want to ask,' said Sheperd.

'Go ahead.'

'Like you said, thousand dollars is a lot of money. If you get it, what you goin' to do with it?'

Herne allowed himself a smile. 'Use it to pay for an operation so's I can play the fiddle again.'

Herne mounted up and walked the horse in the direction of the adobe well. The seven men gathered round it separated out from one another, most of them standing away from the wall and making room for themselves in case Herne meant trouble.

He reined in ten yards away from them and took his time looking them over.

'Any of you know Pierce Latham?'

There were muttered comments and exchanged glances and a few nods of acknowledgement.

'You know me?'

Some nodded their heads again, a few said 'Yeah,' aloud.

'Right, you tell Latham I'm in town and I'm waiting for him. Tell him there's a thousand dollars on his head an' I aim to collect.'

While the men were still open-mouthed, Herne turned his horse and rode off down the street.

Chapter Seven

Pierce Latham rolled off the woman and on to his side. He pulled his left arm out from underneath the folds of her stomach and slapped her on the buttocks, laughing as the flesh shook. He slapped her again and laughed louder when she cried out and then some more when he saw the marks of his hand on her loose skin.

'Damn!' he said with feeling. 'Damn, that was good!'

A sound came from the woman's mouth against the soiled pillow and Pierce Latham looked down at the tousled brown hair and shook his head.

'Damn!' he shouted, swinging back his arm. 'Weren't that the best you had since you first started?'

The woman shifted awkwardly on the bed, trying to avoid the blow she sensed was coming. She succeeded in making Latham miss her behind and strike her hip instead. She called out nonetheless.

Latham grinned and reached for his pants that were lying crumpled on the floor. The woman turned on to her side and looked at him. Rouge was smudged across her face and the pillow both. One breast sagged across the other and folded on to her right arm. There were dark marks under her eyes, lines spreading away from the corners of her mouth. She looked the wrong side of forty and she was twenty-seven.

Latham lit a cigar and tossed the match on to the floor after the chewed-off end.

'Pierce!'

The shout came from the alleyway alongside the house and Latham flinched, then grabbed at the Smith and Wesson sitting in the black leather holster that hung from the bed end.

'Hey, Pierce!'

He moved alongside the window fast and eased back the ragged length of sacking that hung down from a piece of string.

'Pierce!'

When he saw who it was, Latham cursed and yanked his shirt from where it was trapped under one side of the pillow.

'Come up here,' he called through the window and hurriedly finished dressing.

When Cole came in the woman had made no attempt to cover herself. Cole spoke to Latham with both eyes on the woman on the bed.

'What the hell you mean, he's fixin' to collect the thousand dollars on my head?'

Cole was beginning to feel decidedly uncomfortable and he hoped that it wasn't starting to show.

'That was all he said, Pierce, to tell you he was gonna wait till you showed and he'd collect that . . .'

'He a lawman? United States marshal, somethin' like that?'

'No. He . . .' Cole blanched as the woman turned full on to her back and slightly spread her legs.

'Get on with what you're sayin' and get your eyes unstuck from that goddamn whore!'

'Yes, Pierce. Sure. Only . . .'

Latham hit him round the side of the head and he staggered back against the side wall. He caught his breath and ducked as Latham moved closer as if he was going to hit him a second time.

Instead he grabbed hold of Cole's shirt and twisted it tight to his neck. 'Now. Say what you got to say and say it clear.'

'Sure. Sure, Pierce. Like I told you, he don't seem to be no . . . to be no kind of marshal. He's a bounty hunter I guess.'

'Bounty hunter,' exclaimed Latham in disgust, 'that trash!'

'Goes by the name of Herne the . . .'

Latham let go of Cole's shirt and stepped back as if the material had suddenly caught fire.

'Herne? Jed Herne?'

'I guess so. Herne the Hunter, they said.'

Pierce Latham shifted over to the window and finished getting dressed. The look in his eyes was hardening, his movements were cold and precise.

'You . . . know him?' asked Cole softly.

'Yeah.'

'Then you'll be . . . ?'

Latham spun the chamber of his pistol against the palm of his left hand. 'I'll be looking for him. You can see him an' tell him that.'

The naked woman on the bed forgotten, Cole grabbed at the handle of the door, missed, tried again and finally scrambled out of the room.

Latham leant over the woman and pressed the end of the gun barrel against one of her breasts. 'You make sure you ain't busy later on tonight. I'm goin' to have somethin' big to celebrate.' He laughed in her face and a thin line of spittle escaped from his mouth and ran down on to her neck. 'I'm gonna be the man who finally took care of Herne the Hunter!'

Herne cleaned his Colt thoroughly, piece by piece, and put the pistol back together again with a great deal of care. He loaded the chambers and set the gun back in its holster and stood straight. Then he dropped into a gunfighter's crouch and his right arm whirled and suddenly the Colt was back in his hand and ready to fire.

He went through the same practice draw half a dozen times before going down the street to the place called the Swados House. There were some twenty men inside, most of them crowded round the bar at the back of the room, but as soon as Herne entered a hush fell over the place and they parted to let him walk between them.

Herne recognized one man from the days they'd both worked for the railroad company and went over and shook his hand and got a slap on the shoulder and a few words of encouragement in return.

The rest were sullen and silent: Herne was the intruder and he plain as day wasn't welcome but none of them was about to say so himself or attempt to do anything about it.

That was up to Pierce Latham.

Herne had given his intention plain, there was that much to be said for him. He hadn't gone sneaking around back doors the way some bounty hunters would, maybe getting up behind Latham while he was laying with one of the whores he spent so much time with. He'd called Latham out and the man would either have to face up to Herne or ride out and face up to having done that. There wasn't room for doubt in the mind of any person there which of those it would be.

After fifteen minutes the half-breed Mex slid in through the door and Herne's adrenalin began to flow a little faster and he shifted his chair in the far corner of the room so as to be able to watch what the Mex got up to.

Smoke was beginning to thicken but men's voices were still hushed, eager and anxious about what they were sure was going to happen. A group at one of the rickety tables made a gesture towards playing poker but it was little more than that.

Herne called over the Swados and the fat man waddled along behind the trestle table and set his belly against the end barrel.

Herne asked for a whisky: one shot.

'On the house,' said Swados in his thin little voice. 'Didn't know who you was before.'

Herne nodded curtly and took the glass, ripe with the

fat man's thumb print.

'You think he'll come here, Pierce?' Beads of sweat ran easily along the almost bald skull.

Herne gave the fat man a quick look and sat back down.

During the next hour men drifted, slowly, in and out. The air grew more and more congested, until Swados propped the door wide to the street. Herne wondered how close Marshal Sheperd was, waiting to salvage what he could from the pieces. If Herne got hit fatally and maybe Latham, too, then Sheperd would doubtless step in and claim the reward.

Louise.

Herne was angry with himself for thinking of her.

Now.

It was the first time that anything had infiltrated into his mind when he was waiting for a showdown. Herne didn't like it : didn't trust it. The pale face and the dark hair and the turn of her body clung to him. He ordered another whisky and took it down fast, knowing it was the last he could allow himself. Men thought they got faster after a good deal of drink but that was an illusion : a fatal one.

There were others, equally fatal : like young women.

'Herne!'

Conversation in the saloon cut off like someone dashing out a light. Heads swung towards the open doorway, towards the rear corner of the room.

'Herne, you want to see me?'

Herne wiped the palms of both hands down the tops of his pants and stared at the doorway. He knew that the Mex was half-way back down the right side of the room and that he was wearing a pistol holstered high on his left hip, a knife sheathed at the other side.

He tried to figure out what Latham would be carrying. The time he'd seen him out at the Bosque Redondo, he'd worn a Smith and Wesson Schofield .45 in a cutaway holster to the right side and he'd been hefting a sawn-off American

Arms shotgun as back-up.

He wondered if it was still the same: he'd find out.

'You want me, Herne, you come out here an' face me man to man. I ain't walkin' into no trap.'

Herne smiled to himself and touched the smooth butt of his Colt .45 as if for luck.

Something – a bottle? – crashed against the adobe wall of the Swados House and Pierce Latham's angry voice roared after it, uttering threat upon threat.

It sounded as if Latham had been drinking plenty and Herne was both surprised and glad.

'You want that thousand dollars, feller, you're goin' to have to come get it.'

Herne stood up.

Chairs and boots scraped out of his path towards the door.

Herne gave the Mex a hard stare, warning him to keep to his own business, and began to walk towards the door, but keeping clear of a direct line.

He stopped against the wall next to the open doorway. There seemed to be but little light in the street. Fading rectangles from windows and doors, the dull glow of kerosene lamps hung between tents, a three-part full moon and a sprinkling of stars.

Herne knew why Latham wanted him to go out on to the street, he'd be moving out of the light, through it, targeting himself to someone standing back in darkness.

'I ain't goin' out there,' called Herne. 'Not so's you can gun me down the minute I show.'

There was a pause and then Latham's voice, slurred and cocky. 'That's not it, Herne. You come out an' I'll face you fair an' square. I ain't got no cause to be scared of you.' He laughed. 'You're an old man past your time!'

Herne's hand was on the grip of his gun.

'You was makin' a awful lot of noise when I wasn't around, old man. You ain't so damned noisy now.' Latham laughed and another bottle smashed against the wall close enough to the door for pieces of glass to drop down into the light.

'I told you,' said Herne firmly, 'you come in here. I ain't steppin' out.'

Latham laughed mockingly and into the middle of the laugh Herne leapt, ducking low through the doorway, diving across it, hand bringing up his gun as he went. He hit the dirt with his left shoulder and leg and propelled himself forwards. Latham's shotgun roared, orange flared and shot tore at the adobe on either side of the door, flew through the doorway and wounded three men who were standing too close. Herne came up from his rolling motion and into a crouch, his Colt was steady in his hand, Latham was little more than a silhouette in the centre of the street, but a silhouette that was lit with the afterglow of the shotgun burst.

Pierce Latham's hand clawed for the pistol at his leg.

Herne shot him twice, aiming for the bulk of the upper body.

Latham's finger ends knocked against the tip of his pistol butt and he buckled back, staggered three, four steps, folded forward arms jerking to the sides. His head made a strange and unnatural upward turn.

Herne had the hammer of the Colt cocked and his eyes were searching the darkness for any sign of back-up. He watched the doorway of the Swados House but the only thing to emerge was a moan of pain.

Latham was taking a long time getting to his knees.

Herne started, slowly, to walk towards him and, as he did so, Latham pitched forwards, his face slapping against the packed dirt of the street. Herne waited a few moments, then turned him over with his boot.

'Bring a lamp,' he called back towards the saloon.

After a short while, one of the men came out holding a kerosene lantern high. Latham had two wounds in his chest, one a few inches above the heart, the other lower down, towards the stomach. He was bleeding a good deal. Herne bent over him : his breath stank of blood and bad whisky and death.

A footfall spun Herne up and round.

'Easy now.' Marshal Sheperd stepped from shadow.

'I thought,' said Herne, 'you wouldn't be far away.'

'He done?'

'Yeah.'

Seth Sheperd peered down at Latham and nodded. 'In this light that ain't bad shootin'. 'Course, he was drunk an' angry as a bull in a blazin' barn.'

'Marshal,' said Herne, 'those are his problems.'

Sheperd shook his head. 'No more. No more.'

After Mesa, Hondo looked a town with a lot of good points in its favour. Herne dismounted by Harding's store and went in. A couple of women wearing black dresses that swept the sawdust from the floor, looked up from examining dress patterns and gave Herne a haughty look. He didn't blame them : he hadn't bathed or changed his clothes for longer than he cared to recall. But now there was money in the saddle bags slung over his shoulder and a few things he was intending to change.

At first he didn't see Harding hidden behind a couple of flour sacks.

'Well,' the little man said with considerable degree of surprise, 'you haven't come back to lose the rest of your dollars, I suppose.'

Not these, thought Herne, not after what I did to get them.

'No, when you finished attendin' to these ladies, there's a few things I want to buy.'

'Yes, sir!' Harding grinned up at the tall gunman and hustled over to where the women in black were mulling and musing.

Ten minutes later he was able to give Herne his undivided attention. Herne bought a new pair of pants, two shirts, long johns for the winter months just ahead, a new pair of boots and a couple of bandannas. Harding hopped from packet to packet, from bundle to bundle looking happier and happier with each fresh purchase. Usually if folk wanted to buy so much they took the drive into Lincoln or else used one of the mail order catalogues. The little man was almost as happy as if he'd won Herne's money in a game of five-card stud.

'Now,' said Herne, looking at Harding over the top of his pile of packages, 'what I want is some information.'

'Go ahead.'

'First off I need a bath and a shave, then somewhere to eat, and then . . . then I shall be needing somewhere to stay.'

Harding gulped. 'Stay?'

'Sure. Why not?'

'Well . . .' Harding's eyes, bird-like, flicked towards the Colt .45 at Herne's hip. '. . . Hondo don't seem the sort of place for a man who lives . . . who lives . . .'

'By this?' said Herne, patting the butt of the Colt.

'Yes.' Harding flinched as if expecting something to happen.

Nothing did.

'You goin' to tell me what I want to know?'

The little man hurried back around his shop counter and moved to the door. 'Mose Baker's got a barber shop down the street, almost at the end of town. He's got a bath out back, twenty-five cents, all the hot water and soap you can use. He'll give you a good shave and – ' Harding glanced up at the lank strands of dark hair that fell across the top of Herne's broad shoulders – 'and trim your hair. Then as for a place to stay, I don't know what you'd think to it, but trade ain't so good here as you can imagine and there's this room out back here that I've been using . . .'

Herne shook his head. 'I ain't sharin'.'

'No. No, indeed. That wasn't what . . . you see, I can sleep out here in the store. There ain't much of me to stow away and, well, I sure could use a little extra income. Like you said yourself winter's starting to close in and business'll get worse before it gets better.'

'Let me see it,' said Herne.

He saw the room and took it.

'We can agree to keep the stakes the lowest we can, maybe we can get in a little stud every now and again,' said Herne. 'I'm lookin' to have just a mite of time on my hands.'

Harding jumped up and down at the prospect.

Herne left him to it and went off in search of a bath.

'That preacher,' said Herne one evening, between hands, 'the one with the fancy black suit and hat?'

'That Baptist,' said Harding, making the word sound like a description of something much less than pleasant.

'I guess so.'

'What about him?'

'He lives round here, don't he?'

'That's right. Had a place built to the eastern edge of town, close down to the river. Uses it as a church till he can get enough money to get a proper one built. Takes himself a deal too seriously for my liking.'

Herne wasn't considering liking the preacher.

'How's he call himself?'

Harding started to deal. 'You mean reverend or some such?'

'Just his name.'

'Harvey. William, I heard tell.'

Herne picked up the cards and looked at them interestedly. 'That girl of his, she's called Louise, ain't she?'

Harding nodded, yes. He thought for the first time he

was beginning to understand what Herne was up to, but he was holding a good hand and he wasn't about to risk it by opening his mouth at the wrong moment. He simply pushed a dollar piece into the centre of the table and smiled quietly.

Chapter Eight

The day was cold and clear and the tips of the Sierra Blanco were white with snow. Louise rode her horse at a brisk trot over the hard, unbroken ground. Down to her left the flat water of the river was swollen from two weeks of almost constant rain. Now the air was fresh and clean and the land had dried out and it was good to have the freedom to ride wherever she had wanted.

Louise reached out and ran her hand down the animal's hot neck. She smiled and whispered to him, touching her spurs to his flanks and taking him into a gallop.

Up towards the rise of the land slope and then suddenly the man appeared over the ridge, outlined, flat, against the opaque sky.

Louise started and her fear communicated itself to the horse. The man was astride his own mount, watching her. It was several moments of panic before she recognized him.

The horse slowed under her and she pulled on the reins, bringing it back under control, wheeling round to where the man waited.

'I scared you.'

'No, it was my fault. I was silly.'

'I did and I'm sorry for it.'

Herne's voice was strong and gentle. The eyes he looked at her with were calm. Louise noticed that his hair was more kempt than when she'd met him that day outside the store, the stubble freshly shaved from his chin. He wore a bottle-green wool shirt under a tan leather vest and both looked to be new. His wool pants were grey with leather stitched into the insides of the legs for protection when he rode.

He still wore his gun, safety-thong looped over the hammer.

Herne raised the fingers of his right hand to his hat brim and pushed it back a shade. 'You often come out ridin'?'

Louise smiled quickly. 'You should know,' she replied, half-turning her head away.

'Meanin'?'

'You've been watching me for the past four days. Keeping your distance and watching.' She was refusing to look at him at all now, her eyes fixed on some indeterminate object out across the sagebrush.

Herne could think of nothing more to say.

'I didn't expect you, here, so close.'

'You mind?'

The answer came slowly. 'I minded being watched.'

'I'm sorry.'

'It made me feel . . . I don't know . . .' Her shoulders shuddered beneath the blue coat she wore. 'Dirty.'

'But still you came again.'

Her eyes this time showed anger. 'Why shouldn't I ride here? I always ride here.'

She could tell he was trying not to smile at her anger. She wanted to turn her horse away and ride off back home and leave him there. Stupid, stubborn man!

'Why are you watching me all the time?' she asked. 'What are you doing here?'

'Waiting for you.'

She didn't understand: she didn't want to understand: she did.

'What on earth for?'

Herne did smile and Louise thought it was a smile she liked, it made his face look suddenly open and honest – and younger.

'You know,' Herne said.

Louise whirled her head away and called to her horse, giving the reins a quick jerk and setting off down the slope. She kicked at the animal's sides, back into fast trot, not looking round because she knew he would still be there, against the skyline, watching her.

Watching her.

I know why, thought Louise as she rode. I know. I know.

The Hondo had a thin film of ice, like milk, at its edges. The wind blew from the east from dawn past dusk. Herne was wearing a heavy wool coat when Louise saw him, squatting down close by the river bed, and apparently doing nothing. His hat was jammed tight down on his head, a scarf emerging from under the brim and covering his ears.

Louise dismounted fifty yards short of the river and led her horse by the rein. Frost still lay here and there and the ground was slippery for both of them.

She looked at Herne's back, knowing he must be aware of her presence, but he didn't move. Only when she was standing next to him did he look up.

'What are you doing?' Louise asked.

'Waiting for you.'

The Christmas dance and social was held in the preacher's house, it being the biggest in town and the one folk – some folk, those who'd been converted and baptized – were most used to coming to.

Louise and her mother spent days making decorations from paper and painting them, old lengths of ribbon were pressed into service, dresses that Louise had grown out of and which were too worn to be handed down to one of the town girls were cut into strips.

When they weren't tending to the decorations, they were in the kitchen, baking. Meat and potato pies, all manner of pies using fruit they'd bottled in the summer, cakes with icing, cakes without, biscuits and soda crackers and jellies and trifles and custards.

Louise's mother had made her a new dress, white with lace at the collar and cuffs and around the hem. It was buttoned up to the neck with tiny pearl buttons, belted quite tight at the waist. The skirt flared out and Louise had managed to persuade her mother that she could use potato starch on one of her petticoats – as long as her father didn't know.

On the night before she set her hair in curls, using her mother's tongs, and set it in coils of paper.

She was more excited at the prospect of this Christmas dance than she had ever been. Only alone in her bed, the candle snuffed out and her father's cold kiss fading from her cheek, did she allow herself to think why this might be.

There was to be music. Mose Baker, in addition to his skill with the barber's scissors and the undertaker's embalming fluid, could play more than a few tunes on the fiddle. The blacksmith, a Swede whose real name no one could pronounce so they called him Swede, could play the mouth organ. Harding's mother, not wanting her offspring to fall short of a second line in case he grew too tall to carry on the family tradition, had taught him the basic chords of the tenor banjo.

The three musicians arrived early and made a space for themselves in the corner of the long, low room and began tuning up. After a while they started to run through the tunes they could play: reels and polkas and two-steps and lacrymose waltzes.

All of the food was arranged on two groaning tables along one wall.

Louise sat in front of the small mirror in her parents' bedroom and stared at her face in the mirror and asked it questions to which she could get no answers.

The first guests arrived early in the evening, some time after eight, and Louise went running downstairs to greet them, her mother and father already standing there, formally, just inside the door. There was a long pause during which no one else arrived and she was terrified nobody else would. Her father carried in a bowl of hot punch from the kitchen and assured those present that there was almost no alcohol in it, almost none at all. What there was, he assured them, was slipped in by his wife when he wasn't looking. Louise laughed politely with the rest, glad to see her father in such a good mood.

After a little more than an hour, more visitors arrived and then more still and suddenly the room seemed full to overflowing and her parents had left their posts by the door and were mingling and talking. Louise stood close to the musicians with a glass of fruit cup in her hand, tapping her feet to the music and watching what she could of the door.

When they struck up a polka, her father called for silence, quieted the band, waved his hands and insisted that some space was cleared at the centre of the room so that he could dance with his only daughter.

Louise blushed and turned her head.

Her father stood before her and bowed from the waist and asked her if she would honour him with the pleasure of the next dance.

Cole Baker beat time with his fiddle bow and foot and launched into the polka. Louise stepped inside her father's arms and they were whirling, jumping around the floor, his feet sure but heavy, her own scarcely touching the floor, and he seemed to lift her from one step to another.

The company let father and daughter have the first dance to themselves and applauded when it was over.

Harding called a reel and the guests took their partners.

Louise stepped away, hot and flushed, and through the excitement of arms and bobbing heads she saw Herne. He must have come in when she was dancing with her father.

He stood a little way inside the door, looking around the room as though he had yet to see her. He was wearing a dark suit with a watch chain strung across the matching vest – both had been borrowed from Harding's store that day. His hair was brushed and he stood with his hat in his hand.

Louise thought he looked lost. She wanted to go over to him and set him at his ease but she dared not.

When the reel finished, the fiddle player announced a short break for refreshment and repairs to one of his strings and the people clapped and moved towards the food tables. Herne became lost in the crowd which almost at once seemed to expand to fill the entire room.

She saw the little storekeeper push his way between the assorted bodies and then pull Herne away so that they might talk.

Someone next to her began a conversation and Louise turned politely and listened.

The party went on around her, everything happening so fast and yet not connecting with her at all. Her mind hummed with an excitement that was altogether different: her skin hummed with it.

'Louise Ann,' said her mother, stopping and touching her daughter's arm, 'I've never seen you looking as lovely.'

Just six bars into a waltz she felt another touch on her arm and she knew it was him. They slid into the middle of the crowd, Herne holding her almost at arm's length.

He's holding me, Louise thought, annoyed, as if I were china that might break.

As the dance continued and couple wound around couple, they moved closer together. She could feel his fingers on the small of her back, each one of them separate, identifiable, there. His breath across her face as he shifted his head from side to side. His suit jacket was slightly rough beneath her hand. Through it she could feel the warmth of his body. And the hand which held her own . . .

The music had stopped and they were, for seconds, stranded in the middle of the floor.

She was aware of him giving a slight bow in front of her and saying something she failed to understand and turning away. She willed her legs to move but knew they wouldn't. She closed her eyes and found she was walking, too, back to the side of the room.

'Who was that?' her mother asked.

Her father knew.

'Did you invite that man here?'

Her face was stung into redness as if he had slapped her.

'No, Father.'

He moved his arm in such a way that she thought he was going to hit her.

'If you are lying to me . . .'

'William!' said his wife, shocked.

He took hold of Louise's chin with his hand and turned her face so that it was looking up at his own.

'Do you know who that man is?'

Louise could feel her body shaking and she couldn't answer.

'Because I do. That man you were dancing with is a gunfighter, a killer . . .'

'No!'

'Yes! Louise, you have seen him kill.'

Louise's mother wrung her hands and turned away. Now she remembered that morning in Lincoln when they had been visiting the store.

'. . . an outlaw who lives by violence.'

'No, Father.'

He let go of her face and the white marks of his stern fingers were impressed upon her skin.

'No, what, child?'

'He is not an outlaw.'

'He lives by the gun.'

Louise clenched her fingers tight inside her hands. 'He is not wearing a gun now.'

Her mother turned back to them. 'William, people are beginning to pay attention. Can't we discuss this . . .'

'There is nothing to discuss. I will not have a man like that under my roof.'

'Fa . . .' the word faded on Louise's lips.

Her father strode across the room to where Herne was standing.

'You are not welcome in my house.'

Herne looked the preacher in the eye and held his stare

for several moments. Those folk in that part of the room quieted their conversation and tried surreptitiously to see what was going on.

Herne spoke quietly: 'I'll talk with you again.'

Before the preacher could contradict him, Herne strode out of the house.

The preacher had the back of the wagon loaded with planks and he was carting them beyond the existing main street of Hondo, to the place where he intended to build his church. By the time it was ready the street would have expanded that far and the community with it: a church would be needed. His wife would then have the large room in their house to devote entirely to teaching the children who came to her for an hour each day to learn to read and write – and those he shared with her for bible study.

A light fall of snow covered the ground, dusted the planks.

The sky was the colour of oatmeal.

The preacher saw the horse and then, standing some distance off, Herne.

Anger caught in his throat and he reached towards the driving whip beside him on the seat. This gunman, this squalid murderer was defiling the chosen ground for his church. He drew the team to a halt and hauled back on the brake.

'I'll help you unload.'

'No.'

Herne shrugged. 'Heavy work for one man.'

'You've no right here.'

'Why not?' Herne looked around. 'I didn't see no sign.'

'God's sign is here.'

'Because you say so?'

'Yes.'

'And that gives you the right to put me out? To judge? That it? That what your bible tells you?'

The preacher pointed at him accusingly. 'You are a

hired killer. You live by that gun you wear.'

Herne slowly, deliberately unbuckled his gun belt and laid it to the ground.

'What does that prove?'

Herne stepped closer to him, away from the gun. 'Why wear your black? What does that prove? That you're a holy man?'

'It's my heart that's holy.'

'An' mine ain't, that what you're sayin'?'

'Your soul is damned.'

Another pace. 'Don't it say nothin' in that book you carry round with you 'bout folk changin' their ways? Don't that religion of yours allow for that?'

The preacher nodded. 'The lost lamb is more welcome back into the fold than any other.'

Herne looked at him. 'I don't know nothin' 'bout lambs. I got somethin' more important to ask.'

The preacher stared back down, stone-faced.

'I want your permission to come courtin' your daughter.'

The preached seemed for a second to reel back, the next moment the long tail of the whip was flying through the air towards Herne's face. Herne thrust up his left arm and caught at it, letting the whip coil around the sleeve of his thick coat. The fingers of Herne's other hand seized the whip and tore it from the preacher's grasp.

Harvey stumbled forward in the front of the wagon, almost losing his balance and tumbling down over the harness.

Herne threw the whip aside. He was close to the preacher now, close and angry. 'I asked you, I asked you right. Now I'll tell you this. I want Louise for my wife an' I think she wants me. I don't know. I ain't asked her, not yet, I thought that should wait till I spoke with you. I wanted this to be right. For her. I hoped you'd see reason but it looks like reason ain't one of your strong points. So you'd best listen: you forbid me to see her, talk with her, try keepin' her locked in the house and soon as I know what she wants,

I'll take her away from you.' He moved back a step. 'Just take her is all.' He pointed a warning into the preacher's face. 'You think on that a while.'

Louise lay on her bed, head buried in her mother's lap, her mother's hand gently stroking her hair. The girl was quiet now, almost still. She had sobbed herself to silence.

Her mother thought and thought and through the window she saw the sky grow darker and darker. She heard her husband moving around below, his step slow and heavy as though he had suddenly become an old man. She knew that he was sad enough to break.

When she was sure that Louise was sleeping, she slid out from under the girl's head and quietly went to the door, softly walked down the stairs. Her husband's eyes met hers and he knew before she spoke what she was going to say.

The ice on the river had been thick just a week earlier. Louise had walked on it, Herne sitting astride his horse and smiling, warning her that he wasn't going to dive in after her if she fell.

'Jed?'

'Yeah?'

'You did mean what you said?'

''Bout the weddin'?'

'About . . . about your gun.'

Below her the ice gave an almost inaudible creak.

Herne sighed, nodded, got down from his horse. 'Louise, we talked about it and talked and I gave you my word. The day we get married, this Colt goes away in some drawer and I'll not take it out.'

She smiled at him, suddenly radiant again, tried to run off the ice and almost slipped. They both heard the ice groan.

'Hey, Louise!'

'It's all right.'

She skipped on to the river bank and ran into his arms.

All those weeks and he had never kissed her – well, he had kissed her, but not that way, not the way Louise sensed that he should, would.

'As long as I've got you,' Herne said, pressing her tight against him, 'I'll not wear a gun.'

She wriggled away from him, her face flushed with the wind and the crisp air. 'You're wearing one now.'

Herne laughed. 'We ain't married yet.'

'Soon,' she laughed back at him, happy. 'Soon. In the spring.'

Soon, she thought, in the spring.

Her father had been persuaded so far and no further. He still refused adamantly to perform the ceremony himself. A preacher was being sent for from Lincoln. And when the wedding was over, they would go away. Herne had told Louise of a piece of land he knew to the west, in Arizona. Near enough to Tucson for them to be able to get whatever supplies they might need, far enough distant for Herne to lay low and let people forget him, forget his reputation. Begin a new life.

Soon, thought Louise, soon.

And she spent the weeks searching every branch for signs of bud.

Chapter Nine

The letter came through on the stage from Lincoln, but it had taken a detour there from Mesa. Seth Sheperd's hand was shaky and small but the message was clear enough: the Latham brothers, Ezekiel, Damon and Howie, escaped from the state penitentiary, February 3rd, along with their cousin, Billy Dean Latham. Another cousin, Mason, was shot and killed by prison guards after helping them to make their escape.

It was the 28th of February.

The marriage was set for the 20th of March.

Herne thought about it, but he didn't have to think about it long.

Harding was standing uncertainly on tiptoe, attempting to manoeuvre a shoe box from one of the higher shelves, when Herne entered.

'Lo, Jed, can you . . .'

Herne pulled the box free and dropped it down on to the counter. 'Give me some shells, Harding, .45 and .55. Don't waste time.'

The little man looked puzzled, saw the Colt where it had not been for some time, strapped to Herne's leg.

'I thought . . .'

'Shells.'

'Someone ridden into town?' Harding peered past Herne towards the door.

Herne pushed him, firmly enough, back down behind the counter. 'Now.'

Harding nodded. 'Okay, Jed.'

'And a sack of supplies, enough for . . .' Herne shrugged, assessing, 'week, maybe two. Flour and some coffee, some of that dried meat, jerky, beans. I've got my horse to collect from the livery. Have it ready when I get back.'

The storekeeper wet his lips with his tongue, nodded again. He'd had that feeling, like when you're sitting opposite a straight flush and there's no way of knowing other than that itching under your scalp and along the backs of your hands.

Fifteen minutes later Herne was mounted and riding out of town, down towards the Harvey place. Louise was out back, pegging washing on to the line. When she saw Jed riding over, she dropped the clothes back into the basket and ran towards him. Ten yards off she noticed something different, she saw the gun.

'Jed!'

'I know. It's something I've got to do.'

'Jed, you can't, you promised.'

His hands were on her arms, holding her so that she had to look at his face. 'After we're married, I promised then.'

'But you haven't worn that . . . haven't worn a gun for weeks now.'

'I haven't needed to.'

He released her and she turned away, her back almost set against him.

'Why do you need to now?'

Herne hesitated, uncertain how much he should tell her, how much she needed to know.

'Tell me, Jed.'

Louise swung back towards him, one of her hands catching at his wrist, the other held out in front of her, open.

'There's some men, bust out of prison, they'll be looking for me. It don't matter why.' Her eyes questioned him but he shook his head. 'Best I see them before they catch up with me. Away from here.'

'So you can kill them?'

He looked over her head. 'Maybe.'

'Or they kill you.' The other hand curled inside his own.

'I'll be all right.'

'How do you know?'

'I know.'

She backed away, sucking in her wide lower lip, tears fighting at the corners of her eyes. 'Because you're who you are, that's how you know, isn't it? Because you're Herne the Hunter. A fast gun. The fas . . . Oh, Jed!'

She flung herself against him and he held her and rocked her on his body and then lowered his face to hers and when her arms went round his neck he kissed her for a long time.

'Whatever happens,' he said from the saddle, 'I'll be back in time for the wedding. Believe that. Even if you don't hear from me, believe that.'

Watching from the window of the house, Louise's mother saw the anguish in her daughter's face and read the cause. Her breath smeared the glass: he's widowed her before he's married her: the words unheard in the empty room.

Herne didn't know how long it would have taken the Latham boys to have found out about their brother, Pierce, but he figured that it wouldn't have been long. Once the initial heat of pursuit had died down, the rumours and stories would be thick and fast. As soon as they knew what had happened, they'd come after Herne, even if it meant risking getting recaptured. Herne knew their mentality, understood, in part, the way their kind thought.

He rode north, undecided at first whether to strike west towards Mesa or east in the direction of Fort Sumner. The trail between the two was a rough one, winding down across the desert flats away from the Pecos. Roughly midway along it sat Peg-Leg Mary's.

Mary's was a trading post that served for most everything a man riding that trail might need – or think he did. She sold supplies, food and ammunition, served up hot plates of stew and the roughest whisky that ever exploded out of a still. You could lose any money you had at cards and if you didn't mind sharing her with the rats that now and then scuffled about under the sacking in the side barn, you could have Mary's one-eyed sister, Martha. Those times of the month when Martha wasn't available, a man with the gall to ask and the extra dollars to back it up, could avail himself of a little time alone with Peg-Leg herself.

The story ran that Mary had been travelling west in a wagon train that got stuck in the snows high in the Sierra Madre, above the frozen Conejos river. Mary's feet got frozen solid and the circulation threatened to go right up her legs and through the rest of her body. The men poured a couple of bottles of whisky down her, tied her down with ropes, gagged her mouth double, and one of them who'd served on a whaler out of Nantucket amputated both feet an inch above the ankles using a small meat-saw and a clasp knife.

Mary was a gritty woman and the man who crossed her was likely to live to regret it – if live he did.

The main section of the place was adobe, its walls weather-beaten and pitted with bullet scars. More or less attached to the eastern wall was a lean-to barn that more than lived up to its description. A warped hitching rail several yards away from the front needed some half-dozen poles to support it.

As Herne rode in there were four horses tied up.

He knew it was less than likely that he'd ride in on the Lathams so easy, but it was a chance he couldn't afford to overlook.

Herne thumbed the safety thong from round the Colt's hammer and eased the pistol inside its holster. Without touching it, he glanced down at his right boot and at the top of the bayonet handle which nestled there inside a sheath. Herne had been no more than eighteen when he'd ridden through the war between the states along with William Quantrill's raiders. He'd had the bayonet with him ever since. Times it stayed wrapped in one of the saddle blankets he carried with him, others he needed it closer to hand.

He figured this might be one of those times.

Herne rode in quiet, sliding down from the saddle and

taking the horse's reins so as to loop them over the rail. He was doing this when the door opened. Herne dropped the reins, dropped into a crouch, his hand was tight on the smooth butt of his gun.

It was a woman who came out, an oaken bucket resting between shoulder and head with one hand supporting it. Her dress was long and shabby, torn away at the neck, the flowers of the print were almost faded out. She started as soon as she saw Herne, her single eye blinking fast.

'Martha.' Herne spoke low, edged with warning.

She struggled to remember him, distinguish him from the others.

Herne nodded at the riderless horses. 'Who's in there, Martha? Inside?'

'You can go on in, see for yourself, no one special, just a few of the boys passin'.'

She stopped and glanced over her left shoulder, the empty bucket nearly sliding from her hand.

'Who?' demanded Herne. 'Name names.'

Martha gave a wriggle inside her dress. 'Rosso an' Twiley from the Fort. Marv Gladwin. Don't know the other feller's name.'

Herne nodded, relaxed. 'Okay, Martha. You go get your water.'

She gave him a one-sided smile and moved awkwardly away, the heel of one shoe flopping loose as she walked.

Herne finished tethering his horse and went over to the door. He pushed it back and stepped inside faster than normal. Two of the men were leaning against a heap of crates, dealing blackjack down on to the top one. Another, handing over coins to Peg-Leg Mary, whipped round fast, silver pieces slipping between his fingers as he went for his gun.

'Don't!' called Herne and made his own draw as the word was sounding.

Before it had faded the Colt was level in his hand, hammer cocked and ready: the man in front of Mary had but half cleared leather.

'Jesus Christ!' exclaimed the fourth man from a sagging armchair which had somehow found its way into the trading post and never got out. 'If that ain't the quickest I ever see, it's darn close to it. Yes, sir, darn close.'

Sweat stood out on the forehead of the man Herne had drawn on, his fingers seemed to be frozen to the grip of his gun.

'What was you aimin' to do with that?' asked Herne, nodding in the direction of the man's holster.

The mouth opened and the tongue moved but it was seconds before words followed. 'Didn't know who it was. Comin' in quick like that. In back of me. What d'you expect?'

'Who're you expectin'?'

'No one. No one at all. That's . . .' He broke off and glanced each way along the room, seeking assistance. He didn't get it – not from there.

Peg-Leg Mary said: 'If you're aimin' to blow a hole through this feller, let me know first. 'Cause where I'm standin', it's likely to go clear through me first.'

Herne let back the hammer of the Colt and the man in the arm-chair whistled with some relief, or it could have been disappointment. The fingers on the gun butt in front of Herne began to unfreeze. Mary looked her thanks at Herne and hobbled out of the line of fire.

'What's your name?' Herne asked.

'Sheer. Danny Sheer.'

'Headin'?'

'Santa Fe. Santa Fe, mister.'

'From?'

'Been winterin' down round Presidio.'

'Uh-huh.' Herne moved the Colt towards his holster. Almost there, he looked at the man again sharply, asked fast, 'You know the Latham brothers?'

His face remained blank: it was at the corner of Herne's vision, but he could still tell that Peg-Leg Mary's didn't.

'Never heard of 'em.'

'Okay. Finish up here an' move on.'

The sweat that had been gathering on the man's head was now running along the bridge of his nose, a droplet about to fall away.

'Mister,' called the feller in the chair, his voice harsh from too much tobacco and Mary's whisky, 'I heard they bust out of the state pen. Week or so past.'

Herne nodded. 'I heard that, too.'

Peg-Leg Mary pushed a glass in Herne's direction and pointed at the bottle of whisky. Herne shook his head and Mary laughed.

'Still don't take to my whisky, huh, Herne?'

'That's right. I like to live my life without takin' too many risks.'

The man Herne had drawn on muttered his farewells and got out while he was still able.

'Some folk'd say askin' after them Latham boys was a risk in itself,' said Mary. 'Seein' as you finished that brother of theirn.'

'News travels, don't it.'

Mary smiled. 'An' bad quicker'n good.'

'So they say.'

Cautiously, Martha came back in carrying the bucket of water with both hands. Mary got to scolding her for being such a long time and then, when she hurried, aimed blows at her head for slopping water over the floor. Mary had never struck Herne as being house-proud. He watched them for a moment – Peg-Leg Mary hobbling after her one-eyed sister, trying to swat her face with a large, fat hand.

'You men from Fort Sumner?' said Herne, approaching the pair who's been playing blackjack.

Both nodded.

'You Herne?' one of them asked. 'Herne the Hunter?'

'Yeah.'

'Billy rode in not long back. Spoke about you. You was with him down in Lincoln County.'

'That's right.'

Herne set one foot on to a barrel top. 'You up there recent?'

'Couple of days.'

'See anythin' of the Latham boys?'

'No.'

'Not a thing.'

Both shook their heads. Herne let them see his hand shift closer to his gun. 'You wouldn't lie to me now, would you?'

The heads shook again.

'Won't see 'em there, not while Billy's around. Him an' old Ezekiel, they hate one another like poison. That's a fact.'

Herne remembered something the Kid had said once and figured he'd heard the truth.

'Okay.' He moved towards the door. 'Anyone here runs into 'em, you let 'em know I'm lookin' for 'em. Tell 'em, just like I was lookin' for that brother of theirs.'

As he went out of the door, Herne looked quickly back in. Mary's face was composed, but her sister's was all squinted up at the one side and she didn't seem happy at all.

Herne rode away at a steady pace, heading in the direction of Fort Sumner. When he was certain that he was far enough away and that no one was following him, he made a wide loop south and then north again, bringing himself within reach of Peg-Leg Mary's trading post.

He hobbled his horse some distance back and then went forward carefully until he was in a position where he could lie flat and watch who went in and went out.

The pair Martha had identified as Rosso and Twiley came out a little past an hour after Herne arrived back. They mounted up and rode off east, taking the same trail Herne had started out on, back towards the fort.

He had a longer wait for Marv Gladwin. Obviously Marv had got himself so settled in that old arm-chair, or else had drunk so much of Mary's special whisky that he wasn't capable of moving under his own steam. Just when Herne was giving up all hope of him ever quitting the place, Gladwin appeared in the doorway with the air of a man who doesn't trust the outside world. He attempted to walk through the hitching rail, after some difficulty realized that was impossible and clambered over it. It took him six attempts to slot his boot into the stirrup, three to cock his other leg over the saddle. Finally he moved slowly away, west, swaying effortlessly on the animal's back.

If Herne had a good luck charm, he would have used it then. He was trusting to his feelings and nothing more and there were only the sisters' faces to go on. Those and the fact that the post was an ideal place to use as a base for tracking Herne down.

Lacking a rabbit's foot, he lay there thinking about Louise.

They came.

One first and that cautiously, riding in slow from the back so that Herne didn't pick him out until he was almost on the post. He left his horse at the end of the rail and looked around before going in. Two minutes later he reappeared and put his fingers to his mouth. A high, long whistle brought the other three into sight. Everything clear, they rode in at a fast lick, shouting and laughing, rowdy and pleased with themselves. Herne was glad: that would help.

He smiled grimly to himself. If they were still feeling their freedom that way, he'd leave them to stoke the fires a good bit more. Let them drink and holler and get at ease. That was when he'd make his move.

There was no doubt in Herne's mind as to what he had to do. If the Lathams were allowed to live, they would always be a threat to him. Not only to himself, once he was married, but to Louise as well. Putting them back in jail wasn't any use – they'd proved that themselves.

He had to kill them: all.

In his time Herne had killed a good many men: he'd killed them in war and on what the frontier called peace.

There'd been times when he'd been wearing a badge, but mostly he hadn't. He'd killed for causes and killed for money, killed because of circumstance and he'd killed for hate. This would be the first time he would have killed for love.

Four men.

Herne could have used his Sharps and picked off at least two of them when they rode in, possibly three. From that distance and with his skill with the long-barrelled gun it would have been easy.

He wanted to kill them face to face.

Herne had heard of a regulator who used a Claymore rifle and always used it from the longest range possible. He'd do anything he could not to have to see his victim's face when he died. Herne thought maybe he could understand that . . . but he couldn't respect it.

It was time to move.

No!

Martha came through the door, one of the men close behind her. As they went towards the barn, the man – Herne didn't know which one it was – goosed her and she flapped an arm at him playfully. Herne heard her high-toned laugh, over-ridden a few moments later by his. They went round the corner and into the barn.

Herne hesitated long enough for them to be started, then set off himself.

He walked quietly, making a left curve so that he'd arrive at the opposite end from the barn. Softly along the back wall, close to the adobe. Several times, even through the thickness of the wall, he heard a roar of laughter from inside.

The planks of the barn wall were loose and uneven. Through one of the chinks Herne saw the movement of two bodies, the heave and strain. The man lay between Martha's legs, his pants pulled down to his ankles. Herne watched for a moment longer the fleshy buttocks rise and fall. A moan came from one or other of the couple as Herne bent silently and drew the bayonet blade from its sheath.

There was no handle on the barn door, a piece of string knotted through a hole. Herne pulled it. The door creaked and something small scuttled out over his boots. Martha's single eye stared up at Herne and she screamed into the man's shoulder. Her legs were tight about the backs of his knees. The man gasped for air and tried, awkwardly, to turn his head. Herne was little more than a shadow, a shape above him. Over him. Then the blade shifted.

Martha's scream was real.

'Christ, you . . . !'

Herne drove the bayonet through the throat, puncturing the man's windpipe. Pressed down. Twisted.

He clapped his other hand over Martha's mouth and she bit into his fingers.

He moved his hand enough to slap her, quickly, then pressed it back.

The man had stopped struggling, making noises, just a ragged hiss of air from the bared throat. Blood.

Herne slid the blade out and wiped both sides of it on the dead man's shirt. The eyes were open and Herne closed them. He was one of the brothers, Damon or Howie, he wasn't sure which.

No one seemed to have reacted to Martha's scream – probably they had figured it to be part of the fun. She huddled her legs up to her body, tugging at her tattered dress. Her eyes never released Herne's face. She was certain that he would kill her.

Herne bent towards her and set a finger to his lips. 'Stay here. Stay quiet. Don't go back in there till it's over. You understand me?'

Martha nodded, breathing unsteadily.

'Remember,' whispered Herne from the door.

Outside he slipped the bayonet back inside his boot and walked around to the front of the post. One of the men was singing, his voice surprisingly strong and tuneful.

When we arrived in Mexico
I wrote that girl who'd loved me so
I wrote a letter to my dear
But no return word did I hear

Lord pity a girl who won't be true
For a false-hearted love I never knew
I'm goin' back where the bullets fly
And stay on the cow trail till I die

Herne drew his gun and kicked in the door, jumping through the space and turning low. Billy Dean was standing up on a barrel, a bottle in one hand, the other still outstretched in the final gesture of his song. Herne's first shot hammered him into the air, the bottle crashing to the floor as Billy Dean clutched at the sudden pain in the centre of his chest. Ezekiel hollered and grabbed at his holster and was still grabbing when Herne shot him through the side of the neck, an inch beneath the ear. Ezekiel stumbled backwards, falling, sending tables and chairs against one another, screaming.

The other brother lunged for the shotgun that lay on the counter, both hands touching it, starting to turn it. A slug ripped through his left arm, deflecting sideways off the shattered bone. His hand fell away from the shotgun stock and one of his legs slipped under him. He looked Herne in the face and his eyes pleaded mercy: Herne put a bullet through his heart. Latham slammed back against the counter, hung there several seconds, then buckled slowly forward. Herne stepped aside to allow the body room to hit the floor.

Gunsmoke and the stink of cordite mixed with the sour smell of whisky in the long, low room.

Peg-Leg Mary was sitting in the arm-chair by the end wall, hands gripping the sides. There was nothing pleading in her eyes, only a fierce anger.

'You had to kill them all, didn't you?' she said. 'Every poor damned one.'

Herne holstered his gun and stepped over Ezekiel's body.

'And my sister, too?' said Mary.

Herne shook his head. 'She's okay. She's in the barn.'

Peg-Leg Mary wiped a hand across her mouth. 'Herne, you're a heartless bastard. You show yourself in here again and I'll try an' kill you myself, I swear to God on it.'

'Yeah,' said Herne, 'I believe you will.'

At the door he stopped and looked at her again. 'Get what you can for their saddles, guns an' horses.'

It was as though he hadn't spoken. It was time to mount up and ride back to Louise. Time to get married and hang up his gun.

Chapter Ten

It was morning. The sky through the window of Herne's room was shading black into purple, purple into orange, orange yellowing out to a flat, drained white. He was still sitting on the edge of the bed, the whisky bottle was where it had been when the night had begun. Something ached and it was more than the set of his back, the numbness that had entered into his legs.

Someone was coming towards the door. Herne slid the Colt into his hand.

'Jed?'

'Yeah?'

'You awake?'

'Come in and see.'

Tom Lenegan walked in slowly, as though each fresh movement jarred pain through different parts of his body. He was obviously bandaged heavily under his shirt. His face looked white, years older.

'You shouldn't be up an' walking,' said Herne, setting the gun aside.

Tom ignored the remark. 'I've been thinking 'bout what you said. Different things. Can't see any way out.'

'So?'

'I'm riding out there. This morning.'

'The Clayton place?'

'Yes.'

Herne looked doubtful. 'You're goin' to ride in an' tell old man Clayton you're marryin' his daughter.'

'That's it.'

'You know what'll happen?'

'Yes.'

'And if you ride back out of it, then have you figured what your Katie's goin' to think?'

'What's she going to think if I wait till they come after me an' gun me down somewhere without a chance?'

Herne stood up and went to the window. The sky was brightening further, patches of blue seeping through.

'She's not the same as the rest, neither her nor John. They could be different family. There's no love lost between Katie and her pa. None at all.'

'You sure on that?'

Tom nodded. 'Yes.'

Herne still hesitated, his memories of the night strong in his brain. 'Wait up till I get some black coffee,' he said after a few moments, 'I'll ride with you.'

'No.' The word was out of Tom's mouth almost before Herne's offer of help had been made.

'Why not?'

'I've got to do this myself. It's my fight, my quarrel, not yours.'

Herne shook his head. 'You're forgetting something. I was the one who shot Hal Clayton, not you. Besides, you're in no state to go up against four guns.'

'Three.'

'You sure John won't chip in when it comes to it?'

'He won't. I'm positive.'

'That still leaves three.'

'I'll handle it.'

Herne smiled and shook his head. 'Okay, let's say I'm coming along to see how you do it – all right?'

Tom Lenegan struggled with himself, his stubbornness of pride against the sure and certain knowledge that if Herne went with him, he'd be likely to come through and marry Katie, whereas if he didn't . . .

'Well?'

'Thanks, Jed. Thanks.' He shook Herne's hand.

'Okay. Now if you can rustle me up some coffee from

somewhere, I'll wash up. Then we'll ride out.'

First they saw cattle wearing the Circle C brand, then the sails of the windmill and then that gave on to the ranch. A single-storey house in the shape of an L, a high barn and a couple of outhouses, all arranged so that the overall impression was of a nearly closed rectangle. There were fruit trees in a small grove back of the barn. Horses in a corral. Everything looked damned peaceful.

The click of a rifle lever being worked was awful clear.

Tom turned and made a move towards his gun but Herne stopped him fast. 'If he was goin' to shoot one of us in the back he'd've done it. Don't give him no excuse.'

They rode into the middle of the rectangle, Stewart Clayton walking at their backs, the Winchester aimed at the rear of Tom Lenegan's head.

Cyrus Clayton came out of the house with a bull whip in his hands, coiled and mean. Jack was no more than a pace behind him, a pistol strapped to his side.

'You got gall, Tom Lenegan, I'll give you that. Comin' in here like brass an' bringin' that murderin' bastard with you.'

'I came to talk,' said Tom.

Cyrus laughed and flicked the whip out casually, till its tip touched the ground between Lenegan and himself. 'Boy, you ain't got nothin' to say to me, but I got plenty to say to you – an' I'll say it with this.'

He worked the whip and it snapped the air less than a couple of feet in front of Lenegan's face. Tom ducked his head back instinctively and Cyrus laughed again.

Katie came running around the side of the house and stopped short when she saw the confrontation.

Tom looked over at her and smiled, made a gesture telling her not to interfere.

'Get back in the house!' shouted her father.

'No, Pa.'

'Get back!'

She looked at him defiantly, prettily. 'While Tom's here I'm staying put. It concerns me and I've a right to hear what's said.'

For a moment it looked as if Cyrus might turn the whip on his daughter for answering him back so boldly. Instead he hunched his shoulders and then brought back his arm and flicked the bull whip once again towards Lenegan's head. Again Tom Lenegan ducked aside, but this time the whip was a foot closer.

'Better speak up fast,' warned Cyrus Clayton, 'the next one'll take out your eyes.'

'Tell your son to stop pointing that gun at his back,' said Herne, 'then maybe he'll feel more like talking.'

'Shut your mouth!' called Stewart Clayton, but he lowered the rifle just the same.

'Get to it!' snarled Cyrus, his stocky body bristling with anger.

'It's Katie,' said Tom. 'Katie and me. We're goin' to be married.'

Cyrus's round face flushed and then almost as suddenly seemed to drain of any colour. He looked round at his daughter and then back at Tom. If it had been a gun rather than a whip in his hand, he might have shot them both.

'I'm telling you because we didn't want to go behind your back, not any more. You were right to be angry about that. We're going to marry and settle the far end of the valley where my folks live.' He nodded. 'That's all there is to say.'

The words seemed to strangle out of Cyrus Clayton's lips. 'You've caused me to lose my favourite son. Now you think you're going to take my only daughter when you're not worth the price of her spit. You'll do it past my dead body.'

Katie ran forward, placing herself between them.

'Pa, that isn't true. It isn't! Tom's a good man, an honest one. He's worth more than anyone else in the world.'

'Even your own father?' asked Cyrus.

She almost spat the answer back at him. 'Yes! Yes! Perhaps especially my own father!'

He struck out with the bull whip, the thickness close to the handle lashing into the side of the girl's head.

Tom shouted and went for his gun, leaning sideways in the saddle. Behind, Stewart Clayton jumped across to see what was happening, bringing up the rifle at the same time.

Herne sprang down from the saddle, pulling the Colt clear as he was in motion.

Tom's first shot missed the old man and hit Jack in the left arm, the slug tearing through the flesh without hitting the bone. Jack stumbled back inside the house while, in front of him, Cyrus was trying to wield the whip and Katie was pushing herself up from the ground, blood running from a cut beside her ear.

Stewart Clayton fired his Winchester once from the hip, aiming at Tom's back and missing.

'Drop it!' yelled Herne. 'Now!'

Stewart swung the rifle through a short arc and began to squeeze back on the trigger. Herne put a bullet through the space above the rifle barrel and below Stewart's head and shoulders. He bucked backwards as if he'd been punched hard in the chest. The Winchester went off, the slug burying itself harmlessly in the ground.

'Katie! Look out!'

Tom drew a bead on her father as the whip sailed through the air towards him. The lash coiled about Tom's neck and dragged him from the saddle. He half broke his fall with his left arm, but the pain that shot through his chest and thigh was intense.

Jack Clayton reappeared in the doorway, pistol in hand. It levelled at Tom's fallen body.

'Jack!'

Katie jumped towards him as the explosion of a gun shot rocked the air. Her hands went to her face and she fell to her knees.

Jack hit the door frame and fell away like so much dead weight. A .45 slug from Herne's Colt had killed him outright.

'Katie? Katie!'

Tom scrambled towards the girl, wincing at every movement he made. His arms closed on her shoulders and she turned to face him with tears in her eyes and blood splashed across her face.

'Oh, Tom!' she cried and let herself fall forward into his arms. 'Tom, he's dead. He's dead.'

Tom looked over Katie's shoulder. The shot he'd fired as the whip had wrapped itself about his neck had broken open old man Clayton's head and it lay on the porch, spread wide for all to see.

'Tom, oh, Tom.'

'Katie, shush. Hush now, it's all right. It's all over. Over.'

Herne hoped that he was right.

'You'll stay for the wedding?'

Herne shook his head. 'Sorry, Tom.'

'But you must. Katie, tell him. You tell him how sad you'll be if he doesn't stay.'

She touched his arm, her face pretty, almost beautiful except for the traces of pain at the corners of her eyes. 'Please, Jed. I do want you to.'

He put his hand over hers, surprised at how small it felt. 'Katie, I'm sorry. I can't.'

'But . . .' began Tom.

'No. But I'll think about you. You just work hard and be happy. The pair of you.'

He shook Tom warmly by the hand and Katie leaned her face up towards his and kissed him on the stubble at the side of his chin.

An hour later Herne was in the saddle. He knew he was doing the right thing in not staying. There were memories enough already without those that would spring back if he stood up with Tom at the wedding ceremony. He'd ridden back Tucson way thinking there'd been enough time between, but that hadn't been so. He'd let some of his past with Louise up from the box where he kept it locked and now he was going to shut it away again. Maybe one day he'd be able to face it better: look back on those three years as the best he'd known and thank God for giving him Louise, even if it were only for that short time.

He rode south, easing towards the sunset, hoping that for Tom and Katie things would be better.

John Clayton had been in town the day his father and two brothers had been killed in the shoot out at the ranch. He'd ridden back to find their bodies and his sister waiting to tell him what and why. His father's body had lain on the porch, his high-peaked stetson hat thrown some fifteen feet further on and wedged against a post. There were no eyes in his father's head to accuse him, to show him hate or love. John had looked at his father for a long time, then he'd seen to the bodies. He'd ridden back into town and made the arrangements for the funerals. A few days later, he'd put the ranch up for sale and agreed to give half the money to Katie.

Clothes and personal belongings he had burnt, other things were either sold with the ranch or given away.

It was all done efficiently, coldly: even at the funeral John Clayton didn't cry.

When he finally quit the ranch for good it was the day of Katie and Tom's wedding. He rode off with his few possessions packed into his saddle bags and he took nothing that hadn't been his own – except for his father's gun.

John had thought it over for a long time.

He wanted to ride off and forget it, forget what had happened, but he knew that he couldn't. It had to be done and there was no avoiding it: however much he regretted it, he was his father's son.

When he arrived in town there were few people in the street. The wedding was in progress in the church, he'd heard the bells as he'd been riding in.

John tied up the horse and pushed the barrel of the gun at an angle down into the top of his pants, handle towards his right hand. The voices of a hymn drifted out into the street. John looked over at the church door and waited.

THE END

HERNE THE HUNTER 8: CROSS-DRAW
by JOHN J. McLAGLEN

Herne was upon him. A grip like a vice clamped down on his right arm and something that felt like falling rock thudded against his jaw. A fire shot through him as a knee was rammed between his legs and he knew he was falling backwards, knew his mouth was open wide and that what he could hear was the sound of himself screaming. Screaming with pain like some foolish kid . . .

Trouble was brewing when rival ranch owners started using the town of Liberation as their private battleground. When it started, the war between the Double C and the Broken Bar was a cold one. When Herne the Hunter pinned on the deputy Marshal's shield, all of a sudden the war got red hot . . .

0 552 10788 3 60p

HERNE THE HUNTER 9: MASSACRE!
by JOHN McLAGLEN

The tall albino stood by him, looking round at the stillness, calming the horses, checking out that the dead men were really dead. They all were apart from the man with the thirty-six in his stomach and he'd die soon. Whitey put the muzzle of his pistol to the dying man's forehead, gently squeezing the trigger and taking away all the pain and slow passing . . .

Herne the Hunter could never forget it. That dreadful day, way back in '63. When he and Whitey Coburn had ridden along with Quantril's Raiders. William Clarke Quantril who used the Confederate cause to pillage, burn, torture and murder. That dreadful smoke-filled blood-stained day when they stormed the town of Lawrence.

0 552 10834 0 65p

SUDDEN—THE LAW O' THE LARIAT
by OLIVER STRANGE

The word had filtered out that Sudden was dead – and there was no one around to contradict it. Men who had cringed before, swaggered now; others boasted of their encounters with Sudden, the coward.

Only one man stayed quiet: a tall, saturnine fellow wearing two guns tied low. When he heard the rumours, he gave a thin smile; and when someone asked him who he was, he said shortly: 'James Green.' James Green – alias Sudden!

0 552 11442 1 85p

SUDDEN—TROUBLESHOOTER
by FREDERICK H. CHRISTIAN
based upon characters created by Oliver Strange

Lafe Gunnison had passed the word to the homesteaders – quit stealing cattle or take the consequences! Up in the Mesquites, the nesters reacted the only way they knew: they told Gunnison he was a liar and if he showed up in their neck of the woods he'd wind up with a tombstone over his head.

It was trouble – big trouble – all it needed was one small spark to start a war to the death. Only one man could stop it. One man – backed by his courage and the guns he wore. A man with a past, scouring the West for two killers – a man called – Sudden.

0 552 1443 X 85p

CROW 2: WORSE THAN DEATH
by JAMES W. MARVIN

Time was when Crow was a loner, with just his weapons and his horse for company. A time when the snows covered Dakota Territory. When Many Knives led the Shoshone in battle against the whiteman. Against Captain Hetherington and a wagon train of helpless women. A time when Crow joined in the fight on an isolated plateau above the raging Moorcock river and defeat meant something worse than death . . .

0 552 11218 6 75p

THE CALIFORNIOS by LOUIS L'AMOUR

Somewhere, in the mountains of California, there was gold. And the only man who knew where to find that gold was a strange old Indian, known as Juan . . .

The Mulkerins were Irish – a fierce, proud and independent family. But through a run of bad luck they found themselves in the debt of Zeke Wooston – a hard, cruel man who was just waiting to take their ranch if they didn't pay up. It looked as though the Mulkerins were going to have to fight Zeke's gang and the law – until Sean Mulkerin remembered the story of the gold . . .

If only they could find the gold, their troubles would be over . . . but first they had to find Juan – who, it was said, could disappear into thin air – and time was running out – fast . . .

0 552 09696 2 95p

NORTH TO THE RAILS by LOUIS L'AMOUR

He came from the East to buy cattle, to the untamed land where there was no law but a man's raw courage. He came to get his steers to the railroad, not to kill. He was a peaceable man, but when French Williams and the local outlaws mistook him for a victim, there was lead to pay.

0 552 08673 8 95p